BROTHER ENEMY

Books by Robert Elmer

ASTROKIDS

#1 / *The Great Galaxy Goof* #4 / *Miko's Muzzy Mess*
#2 / *The Zero-G Headache* #5 / *About-Face Space Race*
#3 / *Wired Wonder Woof* #6 / *The Cosmic Camp Caper*

PROMISE OF ZION

#1 / *Promise Breaker* #4 / *Brother Enemy*
#2 / *Peace Rebel* #5 / *Freedom Trap*
#3 / *Refugee Treasure*

ADVENTURES DOWN UNDER

#1 / *Escape to Murray River* #5 / *Race to Wallaby Bay*
#2 / *Captive at Kangaroo Springs* #6 / *Firestorm at Kookaburra Station*
#3 / *Rescue at Boomerang Bend* #7 / *Koala Beach Outbreak*
#4 / *Dingo Creek Challenge* #8 / *Panic at Emu Flat*

THE YOUNG UNDERGROUND

#1 / *A Way Through the Sea* #5 / *Chasing the Wind*
#2 / *Beyond the River* #6 / *A Light in the Castle*
#3 / *Into the Flames* #7 / *Follow the Star*
#4 / *Far From the Storm* #8 / *Touch the Sky*

BROTHER ENEMY

ROBERT ELMER

BETHANY HOUSE PUBLISHERS
MINNEAPOLIS, MINNESOTA 55438

Cover illustration by Chris Ellison
Cover design by Lookout Design Group, Inc.

Published by Bethany House Publishers
A Ministry of Bethany Fellowship International
11400 Hampshire Avenue South
Bloomington, Minnesota 55438
www.bethanyhouse.com

Printed in the United States of America by
Bethany Press International, Bloomington, Minnesota 55438

Library of Congress Cataloging-in-Publication Data

Elmer, Robert.
    Brother enemy / by Robert Elmer.
        p. cm. — (Promise of Zion ; 4)
    Summary: The fighting between Jews and Arabs in the chaotic times leading
up to the British withdrawal from Palestine in 1948 brings hardship and danger
to both Dov, the young Jewish refugee from Poland, and Emily, the daughter of
a British officer.
    ISBN 0–7642–2298–8 (pbk.)
    1. Palestine—History—1917–1948—Juvenile fiction. [1. Palestine—
History—1917–1948—Fiction.] I. Title.
    PZ7.E4794 Br   2001
    [Fic]—dc21   2001002520

ROBERT ELMER is the author of several other series for young readers, including ADVENTURES DOWN UNDER and THE YOUNG UNDERGROUND. He got his writing start as a newspaper reporter but has written everything from magazine columns to radio and TV commercials. Now he writes full time from his home in rural northwest Washington state, where he lives with his wife, Ronda, and their three busy teenagers.

CONTENTS

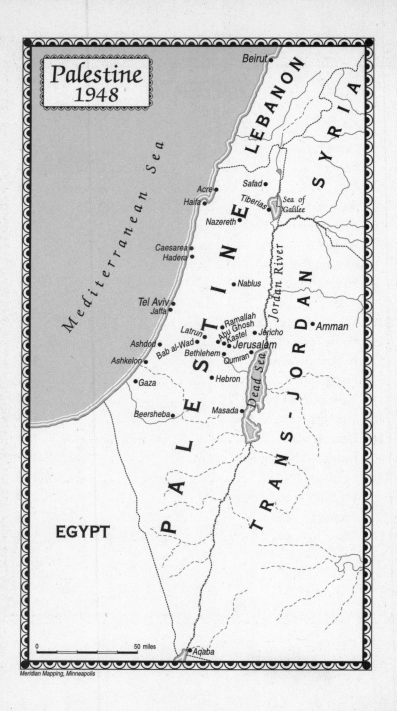

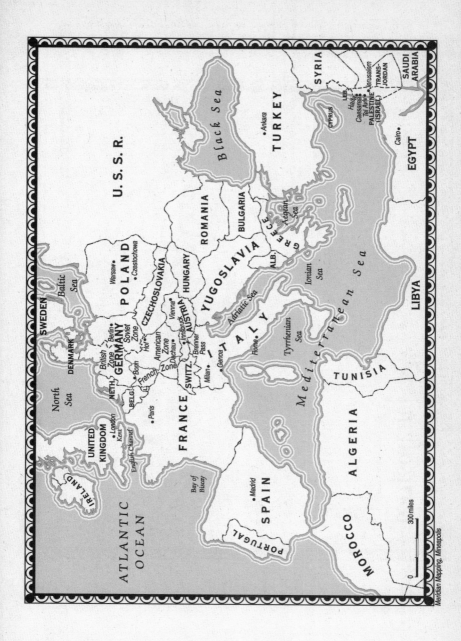

Meridian Mapping, Minneapolis

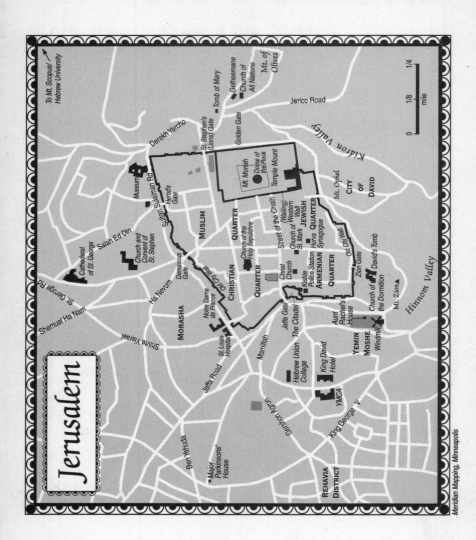

Jerusalem

To Mt. Scopus/
Hebrew University

Tomb of Mary
Gethsemane
Church of
All Nations
Mt. of
Olives

Jerico Road

St. Stephen's
(Lions') Gate
Golden Gate

Derekh Yercho

Dome of
the Rock
Mt. Moriah
Temple Mount

Museum
Herod's
Gate
Sultan Suleiman Rd

MUSLIM
QUARTER

Mt. Ophel
CITY
OF
DAVID

Street of the Chain
(Wailing) Wall
Church of Western
St. Mark Wall
Hurva QUARTER
Synagogue
JEWISH

Kidron Valley

Cathedral
of St. George
Salah Ed Din
Church and
Convent of
St. Stephen

St. George Rd
Shemuel Ha Nam

Ha Nevum
Damascus
Gate
Old City Wall
Church of the
Holy Sepulchre

CHRISTIAN
QUARTER

Christ
Church
Kishle
Police Station
ARMENIAN
QUARTER
Old City Wall
Zion Gate
David's Tomb

Hinnom Valley

Shivte Yisrael
Notre Dame
de France

MORASHA

Jaffa Gate
The Citadel

Aunt
Rachel's
House
Church of
the Dormition
Mt. Zion

Jaffa Road
St. Louis
Hospital
Mamillah

Hebrew Union
College

King David
Hotel

YEMIN
MOSHE
Windmill

Ben Yehuda
Gershon Agron
King George V

Major
Parkinson's
House

YMCA

REHAVIA
DISTRICT

0   1/8   1/4
mile

Meridian Mapping, Minneapolis

LAST PRAYER

Jerusalem
April 7, 1948

I'm not supposed to cry! Not here. Not now.

Dov Zalinski squeezed his eyes shut and leaned against the cold, damp wall built next to the holiest place in the world.

Holy, at least, for the Jews who used to visit it.

Now he knew he was the only Jew in the neighborhood, certainly the only Jew standing there in the narrow-stepped lane, looking up at the enormous square stones of King Herod's wall. And he shuddered to think what would happen if anyone found out he was there.

To his people, it was the *Kotel Hama'aravi*, the Western Wall. The last few square stones remaining of King Herod's temple, left standing in a three- or four-story wall, after everything else had been destroyed by the Romans.

The Wailing Wall. Dov had wondered why people called it that before he had come on a refugee ship to *Eretz Israel*, the land of Zion, several months ago.

But now he understood the name because he *felt* the cries. The Wailing Wall meant more now than the tears of old Jewish women who had come here to press their foreheads to the cold stone and remember what once was. The men in their black hats and overcoats had once huddled on the left side, the women on the right. Dov knew now why so many had come to this place. But that was before—

"He-ya, he-ya!" A toothless old man in a black robe bounced through the street on his donkey, not seeming to care who was in the way. He was coming through.

Dov jumped clear, doing his best to blend in to the Arab neighborhood.

Yes, this wall had once been a place of prayer for his people. But all that had changed about four months ago, after the United Nations' vote to divide Palestine into separate Jewish and Arab sections. Ever since, no Jew had dared come to this Arab part of Old Jerusalem.

So what am I doing here?

Dov glanced nervously at the cluster of crooked Arab homes built right up against the wall. No one seemed to notice him. He looked just like any thirteen-year-old Arab boy.

Or at least he hoped so. He was dark enough, with the help of a little charcoal dust on his cheeks; Mr. Bin-Jazzi's idea. It had brought him this far, through a maze of crowded, narrow streets from Mr. Bin-Jazzi's shop on *Ha Shal-shelet,* the Street of the Chain. For a moment, though, a thought crossed his mind.

Maybe I don't belong here.

Ah, but he did. He reminded himself that this had once been a very Jewish place. He fingered the secret scrap of paper that brought him to the wall and looked for his chance. He would not cry here—not now.

Not for his people.

Not for his city.

Not for his family.

There would be time enough for that later, in a safer place.

He'd already faced the fact that his parents were probably both dead, and his brother, Natan, certainly missing. But right now he felt like a spy on an impossible mission.

For all he knew, Dov was the only one looking for Natan. He *had* to find him! After that, he wasn't sure what else mattered.

A pair of doves perched on a ledge high overhead added their mournful calls. And as the east wind from behind him began to drive an afternoon drizzle against the wall, Dov imagined the quiet sobbing of the stones.

Yes, he *knew* why it was called the Wailing Wall, but to keep his life he had to pretend he didn't. He took another step closer, bent over, and pretended to tie his shoe. The wall loomed not six inches from his head. Would anyone see him?

An Arab woman flicked dirty water his way with her straw broom as she washed her nearby staircase. But Dov ignored her and moved closer to the wall with his two prayers: one on his lips, the other written carefully on a twice-folded scrap of paper. Quickly, he stuffed it into a crack between the huge stones.

There! Dov breathed as he straightened up. He might be the only Jew at the Kotel, but he would not be the last. Of that he was sure.

If God cared.

Do you care? Dov whispered the question into the gray. Then, before anyone could see what he had done, he turned away from the wall, running nearly headfirst into a gang of hard-faced Arab boys.

Emily Parkinson knew her father well enough to know an explosion of anger was coming. She and her mother had seen far too many in the past months not to know.

"This is *precisely* what I've been talking about!" Major Alan Parkinson slammed his fist down on the finely carved dark walnut dining table, brought all the way from England. "Every time they broadcast their rubbish, they simply cause more trouble and stir people up!"

"Dear, dear." Mrs. Parkinson tried to pat her husband's hand, but he shot up and began to stalk around the living room. "It's only a Hebrew radio news broadcast."

"*Only* a radio broadcast, you say!" The red-faced major looked as if he would tear his thinning sandy hair out by the roots. "They *only* have a few guns hidden in their sugar tins, you say. Of course, we can jam the broadcasts, but this *only* makes us look like a bunch of Nazis, for heaven's sake."

"Alan—"

"No. I promise you one thing, Violet. I am going to root out those Jewish *Haganah* radicals if it is the last thing I do before leaving this . . . this place. I shall find their secret transmitter and hold their feet to the fire for as long as His Majesty allows."

Emily knew better than to interrupt when Daddy was giving one of his God-save-the-king speeches.

"Because if these radicals learn nothing else before we leave, they will learn how the British people value proper order and the rule of law! Now, tell me, if you please, is that so unreasonable?"

There. Daddy had spoken. Emily put down her fork and dabbed daintily at the corner of her mouth with her linen napkin, the way her mother had taught her. Her Great Dane, Julian, rested his considerable brown-and-gray jaw on the top of her polished brown loafers, waiting patiently for a handout.

"May I be excused, please?" she whispered.

"And another thing!" Her father appeared not to have noticed her request. "Your mother tells me that you insist on taking Julian out for walks in the city by yourself." He crossed his arms across the chest of his khaki-colored army uniform, waiting for an answer.

"Only once in a while, sir," she squeaked.

He stroked his clean-shaven chin and looked at her, then seemed to catch himself. The real Daddy was in there somewhere, Emily knew. But that man had been hiding for the past months, ever since the United Nations' November 29 decision to divide Palestine had set Arab against Jew with a frightening new fury.

Emily missed the old Daddy, the one who used to smile and laugh. The one who used to go with her and her mother on long walks down Ben Yehuda Street on sunny Sunday afternoons. What had happened to *that* Daddy?

"I'm sorry, princess." Major Parkinson touched her cheek gently. "Your mother and I worry about you. You know what Jerusalem has been like."

Emily knew too well. She rubbed the dark circles under her eyes. She would never get used to the peppery sound of gunshots in the night, no matter how far away they seemed. Lately she had even heard what sounded like rockets, and the occasional *bat-ta-bat-ta-bat-ta* of a machine gun.

But this was *her* city, and she wouldn't allow anyone to take it away from her.

"I know what it's been like, Daddy. But Julian protects me."

He smiled for the first time in what seemed like forever.

"No more lone walks. If you go anywhere, Shlomo has to be with you. Do you understand?"

"But, Daddy—"

Major Parkinson's voice took on a military firmness. "That

is an order. Shlomo will drive you to the new tutor, Miss . . ."

"Pettibone. Miss Pettibone."

"Right. He will drive you there every day as arranged. Anything more, and you will check with your mother or with me. Either that, or you won't be leaving this house at all. Understood?"

Emily swallowed and nodded. She might as well have saluted. At least her parents hadn't sent her away to that horrid boarding school in England yet. But no matter how much they wanted to keep the family together, she didn't know how much longer her time in Jerusalem would last.

"Alan," began Emily's mother, "don't you think we should tell her about—"

"All in good time." Major Parkinson held up his hand. "Perhaps we could discuss it later."

Emily looked from face to face for a clue, but her father's tight lips told her the conversation was jolly well over.

Still she wondered. . . . Tell her about what?

Major Parkinson headed for the living-room door. "And now, if you'll please excuse me, I've asked a couple of chaps from the squadron to meet with me this afternoon."

Emily's mother asked the question with her eyebrows.

"Nothing urgent, dear. Just a little planning session."

Nothing urgent? That didn't explain why they were coming here, rather than the office, on a Wednesday afternoon. So Emily hovered for the next twenty minutes, waiting for her chance to learn more.

"I'll take that in to them," she told her mother in the kitchen. Without waiting for an answer, she slipped her hands under a warm tea tray, deftly balancing the three china cups, a steaming pot of Earl Gray tea, the creamer, and a small sugar bowl. The three officers hardly looked up as she approached their corner of the den.

"I still say we take it out in the middle of the night," said the youngest of the trio. Emily recognized him from her father's office. Sergeant MacDonald.

Take it out? Emily didn't like the sound of those words.

"Well, we do know one thing." Her father commanded the attention of his men as Emily set the tray down quietly behind him. "If we don't officially find and shut down the Haganah radio station soon, the Arabs will most surely blow it up. The station has already received three threats that we know of."

"Probably more that we don't." The sergeant nodded.

"If the Arabs follow through, that would only add to the mayhem." Major Parkinson sounded as if he had made up his mind. "We can't allow it."

"Ahem." Emily cleared her throat politely. "Mum said you gentlemen would like some tea."

They all looked up as if seeing Emily for the first time.

"I see the walls have ears," said the third officer, a man Emily didn't recognize. He didn't stand up or smile, just hid behind a sheaf of official-looking papers.

"Pardon?" Emily didn't like the way he talked as if she weren't there.

"Oh, it's nothing, Emily." Her father smiled and nodded. "Tell your mother thank you."

Emily stood for a moment wondering what else the men were talking about. But to stand there longer would have been impolite. She backed away and turned for the door as her father went on.

"I'm thinking we move sometime next week. Now, all we need to do is . . ."

SECRET JEW

"Who are you?" demanded the tallest of the boys. A typical greeting from one of the gangs of young Arab boys who roamed the narrow streets of Old Jerusalem, making sure their neighborhood streets and alleys remained clear of Jews. The boy couldn't have been much older than Dov—fifteen or sixteen, maybe—but he seemed particularly brave with three friends standing behind him.

"Better to keep one's mouth shut and appear a fool," Mr. Bin-Jazzi had once told him, *"than to open one's mouth and remove all doubt."*

"Did Mohammed say that?" Dov had asked the storekeeper. Mr. Bin-Jazzi had smiled, and of course Dov knew better. His boss and friend was a Christian, a believer in *Isa al-Masih,* as the Arab believers called the Messiah. But Isa al-Masih had not said it, either.

"Mark Twain," Mr. Bin-Jazzi had said. "An American writer."

Dov was willing to bet no one in this street gang had ever heard of Mr. Mark Twain, either. And he was sure he didn't want to be the one to introduce them.

Instead, he put on his I'm-mute act, pointing to his open mouth and shaking his head to mean "I can't speak." He thought it was worth a try.

"What's wrong with you?" asked the lead boy, or so Dov thought he understood. He had picked up quite a few Arabic phrases in the past months, thanks to Mr. Bin-Jazzi's insistence on daily lessons. So now Dov understood more than he could say, and certainly more than he could read. But he wasn't about to utter a word of the kindergarten Arabic he'd learned. A single word would have been enough to signal to everyone in the neighborhood who he really was.

I'm a Jew, not an Arab! They'll think I'm a spy!

"He can't talk, Gamal," said one of the others. "Just a mute. Let's go."

"No. He has a mouth. A tongue. He can speak."

Gamal looked curiously at Dov, as if trying to decide what color hid behind Dov's crude rain-streaked makeup. Two boys had come around to block him against the wall, and the back of Dov's leg blocked his little prayer note from sight. It stayed partly hidden in a crack between stones, where hundreds of notes had once been wedged.

"Or did someone cut out his tongue?" The gang's leader went on.

Dov shivered at what he thought Gamal had said and turned to the right. Even if he couldn't understand all the words, he could follow the meaning and the tone.

And it sounded evil. They would not let him go until they'd had their sport.

"Come on," said Gamal. "Open up."

But Dov wasn't about to open his mouth to Gamal or to anyone. The last time he'd done that, during the war, a German concentration camp doctor had nearly choked him with a flat wooden stick.

Never again.

"Oh, a stubborn one." The leader leaned closer, a fire kindled in his dark eyes.

Dov clenched his fists, ready for what he was sure was to come.

"Come on, Gamal." The boy at Dov's left turned to their leader. "Forget it."

But Gamal brushed them aside and said something else, this time too fast for Dov to follow. Something about a tongue. Maybe he wanted to see if Dov had one.

Dov knew he had to get away, so he jerked to the right, leading with his elbow. He hadn't meant to catch the third boy's stomach, but—

"Ohh!" grunted the boy, gripping his stomach. He crumbled to the side, but the fourth boy took his place. If this was turning into a rumble, the odds were still three to one in the gang's favor.

"Hey, you!" Gamal lunged.

In the tussle that followed, Dov did his best to even the odds. But this gang had obviously done their share of street fighting. One grabbed Dov's left arm and twisted hard. Gamal grabbed his right.

"Hold still, kid!" he ordered. Dov squirmed with all his strength, but it wasn't enough. His sleeve ripped, and they shoved him against the ancient wall. His head snapped back and thunked against solid stone. Any harder, and his head would have cracked like one of the shriveled watermelons in the Arab *suq*, the street market.

That's when Gamal's expression changed.

"Well, well. Would you look at this."

Dov knew without looking what they had discovered. But no matter how hard he struggled, there was no getting free of the double grip. It was too late.

"A Jew. Look at the number on his arm."

By this time Dov felt certain his life was over. A mob had started to gather around. Mostly young street toughs like Gamal and his friends, plus a few older men, as well. Some women stood around the edges, calling, chattering. All to see the unfortunate Jew who had wandered into the wrong Old-City neighborhood at the wrong time. Now they would bring an end to this sin, he was sure. Dov had heard about what some of the mobs had done recently.

"What's this, Gamal?" called one. "A Jew, come to pray?"

Someone spat at him. And now Dov was thankful for the sweet gray drizzle falling from the sky, almost as if God himself were wiping the tears from his cheeks.

A few others added their own comments, but Mr. Bin-Jazzi had not taught him how to curse in Arabic and Dov was glad he couldn't understand most of the words. He was pretty sure he did not want to.

Lord, he found himself praying as the noise of the mob grew louder. Strangely enough, he didn't feel scared. Only disappointed.

I'm not done yet, he prayed. *I have someone to find first.*

He had come all this way—out of the Nazi death camps of Europe, the ashes of Poland—for this? Would God cheat him out of seeing the end of the story?

Dov would have been ready for blows, for a kick in the ribs, a slap in the face. But he wasn't ready for the water, full in his face. The dirty water caught them all at the same time.

"Hey!" shouted Gamal, and his gang loosened their grip on Dov's arms as they sputtered and turned. "What—"

Dov knew he wouldn't have another chance. He ducked and fell to his knees as the shoulder-to-shoulder crowd swayed and shouted in surprise at the sudden attack. Above and behind him, he glanced up for a moment to see the woman who had been sweeping her steps. She flew in with a broom, swinging her weapon and screaming.

"Animals! I'll get you!"

But who was the animal? Him? Them?

I'll let them decide. Dov crawled through the mud and the crowd, looking for an opening. They had to see him coming through, but by this time everyone seemed more interested in the joust by the wall. A crazy woman with a broom against a street gang. A few people even laughed and cheered.

Let me through. Please! As soon as he could, Dov stood and pushed his way through the crowd. He stumbled backward, turned, and ran as fast as his legs would carry him. It didn't matter to where. Just away from the crowd, away from the gang.

Around an alley corner, the crowd sounds fell away behind him. He leaned for a moment against the mossy shade of a stone building, his chest heaving. And he wondered.

Is this what an answered prayer is like?

Maybe the start of an answer, he finally decided. And he also decided against reminding God about the note in the wall, at least not so soon after he had placed it there. After all, Dov still wasn't quite used to addressing the Almighty. He didn't want to come across like a pest. Of that much, he was sure.

The crowd cheered once more, and Dov thought he heard footsteps running his way.

Which way now? he asked himself. Left would take him back to the safety of Mr. Bin-Jazzi's shop. The place he had called home since he had arrived in the Old City.

No, he shook his head, *I've already told him good-bye.* After all, the shop wasn't safe anymore. Not with so many gangs. Nowhere in the Muslim Quarter was safe anymore. Not for him. And not for Mr. Bin-Jazzi if he again allowed a Jewish boy under his roof—as he had up until that morning.

So it was decided. It was time to look for the rest of the answer to his prayer.

Dov waited until the runners had passed, then hurried out of the alley. If he stayed on the main street—*El-Wad*—it would eventually take him through the Damascus Gate and out of the Old City. Yes. That was the way out.

He lowered his head and ran.

LAST HOPE

Dov didn't slow down until he had made it all the way down busy El-Wad and out Damascus Gate. He glanced at the water seller by the gate for just a moment, watching him pour a drink from the long brass jug strapped to his back. Dov swallowed hard and checked his pockets, knowing they were empty. In his mind, he went through his choices one more time.

I suppose I could have run back to Mr. Bin-Jazzi. He shook his head. *No, that's not an option. I already decided it wasn't. He doesn't need more trouble.*

A drab, olive-colored British army truck rumbled by, leaving a choking black cloud behind. Dov turned his head and pressed his nose to his sleeve to breathe.

Or I could find Emily Parkinson. He paused for a moment. She wasn't as bad as he'd thought when he'd first met her, after arriving in Palestine. But her father *was* a British army officer, after all. And that made it awkward for a *ma'apil* like himself—an illegal immigrant.

Yes, he argued with himself, *but who says I'm illegal?*

The British, who were going home within weeks? Did *they*

say he was illegal? The Jewish people who had helped him when he first swam ashore said just the opposite. Still, he did have one other choice.

I could go back to the Haganah house in the Yemin Moshe neighborhood. The safe house run by Jewish freedom fighters he'd heard about from the *gabbai* at Hurva Synagogue. He had tried his best to find refuge in the house once before, several months ago. British guards in the neighborhood had made it impossible. Maybe things would be different this time. Maybe the Haganah could help answer his prayer.

Either that, or he could sleep on the street. And with the drizzle still rinsing his skin, that didn't feel like much of an option.

"Yemin Moshe." He liked the sound of the name, and he let it roll off his tongue again and again as he climbed the steep hill a half hour later.

Dov kept his eyes wide open for trouble. He sniffed the air for the telltale cigarette smoke that had warned him once of two British guards.

He could smell nothing but the damp earth and well-watered Yemin Moshe flower boxes. The rainwashed gravel lanes between whitewashed Mediterranean-style homes looked quiet enough, except for three small children bouncing a ball on garden-path puddles.

All clear?

He decided not to go to the back door this time, the way he'd been told to do at Hurva Synagogue. He would simply wait for dark, which would be easy; it was nearly dark already.

Two hours later Dov was standing in front of Number 3

Malki Street, looking over his shoulder as he knocked. A soft yellow light glowed from under the door, so he knew someone was home. After two more quiet knocks, he stood facing a striking, dark-haired young woman. She was much too young to be his missing mother.

"May I help you?" she asked in Hebrew, then tipped her head to the side and lifted her dark eyebrows in a question. She had a different way of speaking, an accent he couldn't identify. She scooped a wave of black hair from her forehead and tucked it into a fashionable braid.

"I . . . I . . ." Dov's mouth went dry, though the rest of him was well watered. He wiped the rain off his forehead with his soggy, ripped sleeve. "That is, I was told you might be able to help me . . ."

His voice trailed off, and he wondered how beat up he looked and how much he should say. Now that he was here, he wasn't so sure. Surely it wouldn't be so easy getting help from the Haganah. If this woman *was* Haganah.

"You look . . ." she began. When she leaned out her door, her shining dark eyes darted quickly from side to side. "You look as if you'd better come in and dry off."

Yes, that was what he'd come for. Still, it was hard to make his legs move.

"Anthony!" the pretty young woman called out as she pulled Dov inside and shut the heavy front door. "We have a visitor."

Dov decided from the start that he would not mention the first time he'd come by this home, more than four months ago.

"Won't you sit down?" She motioned toward a worn but comfortable-looking couch in the small front living room. "My name is Rachel Parkinson. And you are . . . ?"

Dov was about to sit down, but the name froze him in place.

Parkinson? As in *Emily* Parkinson? No, it had to be another Parkinson. And why would a Jewish woman have such an English name?

"Rachel?" A man came striding in from the back room, dish towel in hand. "Oh, hullo. What's this?"

He looked a bit older than his wife, perhaps thirty. A younger version of Emily's father, but with a full head of blond hair and plenty of worry wrinkles to go around. Now there was no doubt of this couple's relation to Emily. And he spoke English.

Dov shook his hand. "My name is Dov Zalinski," Dov told them. "From Poland."

"Looks as if you've been in some sort of scuffle," noted Anthony.

His wife shot him a look. "You speak very good English, Dov Zalinski from Poland." It occurred to Dov that she spoke English like an American.

"My mother," Dov replied, as if that explained everything. "She is . . . that is, she *was* from England."

Rachel nodded as if she understood. Maybe she did. Most families had lost loved ones in the war—especially Jewish families.

"So your parents are not . . ." Rachel crossed her arms as she asked the obvious question. "I mean, you are alone?"

Dov nodded. "I think my mother died in the Nazi death camps or the Warsaw ghetto. I'm not sure." Dov had never said the words before. But now it didn't seem to matter that he was speaking them to a stranger. "I know my father died in the English camp on Cyprus. All he wanted was to come here to Palestine, like me, but the British . . ."

Dov paused when he noticed Anthony glancing at his wife with a frown.

"Go ahead," said the man. "I've heard it before, I'm afraid."

"The British killed my father in their camp. Well, they didn't *kill* him. But if they had just let him come to this land . . ."

"I am so sorry." The look in Rachel's eyes told him she really was.

Dov decided to spill out the rest of his story. His cheeks flushed red. "He told me you could help someone like me."

"He?" Anthony wanted to know.

"The gabbai from Hurva Synagogue." He sighed. "I'm looking for my older brother. He still lives. I have to find him. He's all I have left." He paused. "But I don't know where to look anymore. You Haganah, maybe you can help me."

"Wait just a moment." Anthony held up his hands. "What makes you think we have anything to do with the Haganah?"

"The gabbai said—"

"My wife is an American, a tutor at the university before all the . . . troubles. I'm from England. A journalist."

Dov gulped. He knew he was in the right place. Wasn't he?

"But I thought—" He looked from Rachel to Anthony and back, just as the front door burst open with a mighty crash.

"Down!" barked a man. "Everyone down on the floor!"

"Shlomo, what are you going to do after all the British leave?" Emily balanced on top of her Latin book in the middle of the wide bench seat in the back of her father's car, trying to see the driver's face in the rearview mirror. All she could make out were Shlomo's unsearchable black eyes.

He didn't answer right away. "We will do whatever it takes to defend ourselves, of course."

By "we" he meant the Jews. Even though Shlomo was Jewish, he had served her father as a driver for as long as she could remember. But somehow Emily could not imagine their middle-aged driver with a rifle in his hand, marching, fighting, or shooting. It didn't seem dignified enough for someone like Shlomo. He turned right just after they had passed the French Consulate.

"But what about right now, Shlomo?" She couldn't help wondering, not with everything that was going on around them.

"Eh?" He didn't follow.

"I mean, *before* the British leave Palestine. Are you in the Haganah?"

Emily brought her hand to her lips at the suddenly dark look in her driver's eyes and wished she could take back the question that had just popped out. Shlomo had always been nice to her. Polite. Protecting. Almost like an uncle. Now, perhaps, she had crossed an invisible line.

"You should not ask such questions, Miss Emily."

But she noticed he did not say yes or no. Perhaps just one more question wouldn't hurt.

"Well, then, I don't suppose you've heard that Haganah shortwave radio station lately, have you? Daddy was quite upset about it. He says they're stirring people up, giving only one side of things, making people more afraid than they should be. What do you think?"

They drove another block in silence before Shlomo finally pulled the car to the side of the road, yanked up the emergency brake, and turned around in his seat.

"Do you really want to know what I think, Miss Emily?"

She swallowed hard and nodded. Maybe she oughtn't to have asked, after all.

"I think that a young girl like you should concentrate on her Latin lessons and on memorizing the poetry of Keats and Byron." His gaze was steady and his jaw tense. "I think this city is no place for a young English girl. And I think if you were my daughter, you would have been sent home to England long ago."

"Home to England? But Jerusalem is my home!" she objected. "I would just as soon be sent to Siberia."

He shook his head. "Jerusalem is a battlefield. And the shooting you hear every night? The Arab shelling from Sheikh Jarrah? This is only the beginning. The Arabs blow up a few houses now, but you just wait until the British soldiers leave. The countries around us will invade, I'm sure of it."

"But my parents say—"

"Yes, and speaking of your parents, have you noticed the difference in your mother lately?"

Emily was caught off guard by the question. She had never heard Shlomo speak this way before.

"Forgive my saying so, Miss Emily, but your lovely house is a prison. She never leaves. Afraid of the shooting, yes? And who can blame her?"

Emily didn't answer.

"You ask what I think? I think you should consider your mother, for a change. Or perhaps you have forgotten the fourth commandment? You Christians do follow the commandments, do you not?"

"Honor thy—" Emily began.

"Father and thy mother." He interrupted to finish the verse for her. "I'm sure you remember your Sunday school lessons."

By that time all the wind had left Emily's sails. She was certainly sorry she had begun this conversation.

And Shlomo wasn't even finished yet. "You asked what I

think, Miss Emily. Well, do you want to know what else I think? I think we should not discuss this again. And I think that you should get out of the car now."

Emily's jaw had already dropped through the floor. Had she heard Shlomo right? Surely he didn't really want her to walk home by herself, did he? Where had they stopped? For once, she was clueless.

"The yarn." He pointed to the brown paper sack on the seat next to her. "For your aunt Rachel, remember? We're here."

"Oh yes, of course." Emily grabbed the sack, glanced out the window, and slid out the back door. If there was one thing she was good at, it was a quick recovery. "How silly of me to forget. I'll be right back."

Emily skipped away as fast as she could, down the wide stone stairways and through the neat, narrow lanes of her aunt and uncle's Yemin Moshe neighborhood.

"Home to England . . ." Shlomo's words echoed in her ears, but they sounded false. Home was not England. It never had been, except when she was very small, and she could hardly remember that. But if home was not Jerusalem, either, then where *was* home? The question cut like a knife.

Overhead, a dark slate sky threatened more rain. And the heavy early-evening air smelled like wet orange blossoms. But she had no time for smelling flowers.

I hope Aunt Rachel will be there. She quickened her step down the hill as she neared the corner of Malki Street, still clutching the skein of yellow yarn her mother had given them to drop off on their way back from the tutor's.

STRANGE MEETING

4

Dov did his best to breathe through the pillow. He'd seen a big man holding what looked like a gun in his hand—but everything had happened in a blur. Now he fought for breath as the intruder kept a boot on the back of his neck.

"You tell me what I need to know," said a rough voice in heavily accented English, "and no one gets hurt. We start with the boy."

Start wherever you want, Dov wanted to shout. *Just let me breathe!*

"Tristan—" Rachel objected. Wasn't her husband's name Anthony?

Dov tried to hook an arm around his attacker's leg, tried to kick, tried to wriggle free. *You'll be sorry*, Dov threatened the elephant on his back. *I'll teach you a lesson.*

But he couldn't move, couldn't see. His face was full of lint from the sofa cushion, and he felt more like a doormat than anything else.

"Do these people help illegal refugees?" demanded the man. "Tell me now!"

By this time Dov guessed he had to be some kind of immigration police, an officer, perhaps.

"Mmooph." The cushion tasted like stale washrags. Dov tried to shake his head no, but he couldn't move.

"This is your only chance, kid. I don't care about little fish like you. Tell me and I let you go."

My only chance? For just a moment Dov wondered what would happen if he answered. Would the intruder really let him go?

"I'm counting to three," threatened the man. "And then—"

Should Dov tell what he knew?

"One . . ."

No. They had opened their doors to him.

"Two . . ."

Even if they *were* Haganah, or if they were helping illegal refugees like him, Dov knew he could not betray Rachel and Anthony.

"Three!"

"I can't tell you anything!" Dov yelled into the sofa cushion. "I have nothing to say."

"Tristan, that's quite enough. Tristan!" Rachel Parkinson raised her voice over the chaos once more. "Are you satisfied? Please! This is outrageous."

"All right, all right." The man's voice softened, and Dov felt himself turned onto his back like a roast over a fire. He looked up into the grinning face of a broad-shouldered, red-haired young man wearing normal street clothing. "I'll let him go."

Tristan, if that's what his name was, held out his hand so Dov could get up.

"There, now. No harm done, eh?"

Dov ignored the hand, got up on the sofa, and rubbed the boot print in the back of his neck. What was going on here?

"Tristan, that is the last time you will play this ridiculous game, do you hear me?" Now it was Rachel's turn to go on the offensive. She slipped over to Dov's side and sat down but kept her gaze leveled at the man standing there. "Promise me you won't do this again."

"Ah, but, Rachel—"

"But Rachel nothing. You scared this boy half to death, and for what?"

"You know what could happen." He started to replace his gun under the belt of his trousers, but Rachel grabbed it out of his hands.

"Are you still carrying this idiotic toy gun around?" she asked him, holding the gun up to the light. Now that Dov had a good look, he could see for himself it wasn't real.

"Comes in handy sometimes." He took it back.

"I'm afraid it'll get you killed someday."

"You worry too much."

She dismissed his protests with a wave of her hand.

"I apologize for our 'friend' Tristan," she told Dov. "I'm afraid he's a bit of an actor, as you can see. He thinks he has to protect us from spies and infiltrators and such. But what are you doing here tonight, Tristan?"

The man shrugged. "I was just wanting to talk to Anthony about some problems with the transmitter. I peeked in and noticed you had a new visitor. Thought I'd help you out again."

"Help us out?" Rachel wasn't satisfied. "When has your act ever helped us out? What about the time you broke that poor fellow's ribs?"

"Now, that was an accident. And a long time ago."

"Three months is a long time?"

Anthony snapped his dish towel at Tristan's backside, and the newcomer yelped.

"If you want to help, you can help me out with the rest of the dishes. But you'd better apologize to our guest. He may be staying with us for a while."

"Sure, I'll help, if that's where the food is." Tristan again stuck his hand out to Dov. "No hard feelings, lad?"

Dov thought for a moment before taking the big fellow's hand. And what had Anthony said? He'd be *staying*? He felt himself pulled to his feet just as they heard a sharp knock on the front door.

"Are we expecting anyone else?" Anthony quizzed his wife.

She shook her head quickly.

"Say, I'll just hide behind the kitchen door," whispered Tristan, "and then—"

"Absolutely not!" Rachel and Anthony answered in chorus.

"You've done enough damage for one evening," Anthony told his friend as he went for the door.

✡ ✡ ✡

Emily paused after she'd knocked the first time. For just a moment she wondered if perhaps she had absently knocked on the wrong door. Of course, she'd visited hundreds of times, but . . .

Whose voice is that? The man didn't sound like Uncle Anthony.

But no, it was Number 3, all right. Finally Uncle Anthony opened up the door, but only a crack.

"It's me," she said, holding out her mother's gift. "Mum said we should drop this by on our way home."

"Oh, it's only you." Her uncle smiled and sighed as he pulled back the door. "Rachel, it's Emily. Says she has something for you."

"Come in, Em!" Rachel called somewhere inside. But Emily hardly heard as she stared at the boy sitting on her aunt's sofa, rubbing his neck.

"*You!*" She couldn't help pointing. "What are *you* doing here?"

Anthony wrinkled his brow and stepped back from the door. "I take it you two are acquainted?"

"I never thought I'd see you again, Dov." Emily barely whispered the words. "At least, not so soon."

He stared back at her, then at her aunt Rachel and uncle Anthony. A big red-haired man she didn't recognize leaned against the kitchen doorframe, looking away.

"I *knew* there was some connection to you." Dov finally answered. "I knew when Rachel said her name was Parkinson. And Anthony looks—"

"She's my aunt." Emily did her best to explain. "And Uncle Anthony is my father's brother. But now you've met, have you? How?" She shook her head in confusion as her aunt stepped up to meet her.

"He needs work and perhaps a place to stay," said her aunt. "Right, Dov?"

Dov nodded and turned to Emily. "I've been staying with Mr. Bin . . . you know. But—"

In the distance Emily heard a car horn blaring once, then again. She clapped her hands together.

"Oh dear, I'm sorry. Shlomo is waiting for me. I was just supposed to run this in. If I don't return immediately, he'll send the police after me." She knew it was true, especially after the latest lectures from her father.

"Tell your mother thank you for me." Aunt Rachel took the yarn. "And do come back when you have more time to chat."

Emily nodded and backed away, then hesitated for just a moment.

"It was good to see you again, Dov. Er, you're still looking for Natan, aren't you?"

Dov nodded, and Emily turned to go.

"Good luck, then, with finding your brother," she whispered.

From a distance, up the hill, the car horn sounded once more. She turned and hurried outside.

COUNTDOWN TO
DANGER

5

Emily awoke the next morning to the sound of a teakettle whistling and her mother clinking cups and saucers in the kitchen. Rubbing the sleep out of her eyes, she tugged on her robe and padded down the stairs.

"Mum?" Emily peeped around the corner. "You're up early."

She nearly gasped when her mother turned to look. Normally, Mrs. Parkinson was prim and made up, almost regal looking. Even early in the morning, her hair was usually pinned up carefully, every hair in place, and she might be wearing her favorite pearl necklace or ruby brooch. In fact, more than once Emily had imagined her mother was the queen, and she herself a princess.

No one would make that mistake *this* morning. Mrs. Parkinson peered at her daughter with puffy red eyes and a sunken, hollow expression.

"Oh, Mum, are you quite all right?" Emily knew that wasn't the proper way to greet her mother. It just came out that way.

Mrs. Parkinson nodded. "I'm afraid I didn't sleep much last night, again."

"You too?" Emily knew why without asking. The nighttime shootings had started late last November. Now, in April, she was afraid they both wore dark circles under their eyes.

Emily's mother nodded, then turned back to her tea.

"You didn't have to get up, dear. You need your sleep."

"It's all right." Emily put her arm around her mother, which she could do now that she had grown at least a couple of inches in the last few months. She was tall enough to give her mother a good hug, if that's what she needed. And it looked as if her mother certainly needed a hug just then.

"Listen, Mum, I've a grand idea. You need to get out. *We* need to get out."

Mrs. Parkinson started to shake her head and turn away, but Emily held her gently by the shoulders.

"Please, Mum? It would do us both good. It'll be a lovely day. I don't have lessons until this afternoon. Shlomo could drive us downtown, the way he used to. Perhaps you could buy a coat at Mandelbaum Furs, or a hat at Spinney's, or . . . or something."

"There are no hats in this country anymore. At least, no fashionable ones."

"Then a dress. A purse. Anything. Just you and me. We'll go shopping, the same way we'll do if—" she took a deep breath—"*when* we go back to England."

When we go back to England. Emily hadn't dared say that before, and what else had she and her mother argued about lately? Going back. Staying here. Going back. She'd cried too many tears to count. But strangely enough, as Emily surrendered the contest, she felt better than she'd imagined. She guessed perhaps Shlomo's words had shaken her enough to let her see how selfish she had really become.

"What did you say, dear?" Emily's mother probably couldn't

believe what she had heard, either.

"I said, when we get back to England, I daresay we'll still go out shopping together, won't we?" Emily tried to smile.

Her mother seemed to brighten at the sound of Emily finally talking about England. She looked up at her daughter with a shadow of the sparkle she used to carry in her eyes.

"Or perhaps, Mum, you'd rather I went out alone?"

"I'll get Shlomo." Her mother put down the kettle, then stopped. "But, oh dear, I'm not dressed yet, am I?"

Mrs. Parkinson smiled for the first time in months. And for the next hour, it seemed to Emily her mother made an extra effort to chat about normal things like hairstyles or the latest Frank Sinatra hit song.

So this is normal, Emily thought as they drove down Ben Yehuda Street, in one the busiest downtown blocks of the New City. She gazed out the car window at passing shops: Riesel Shoes. Barnett Brothers & Borchard, Ltd. Levy's Suits for Men. Already, early-morning shoppers were beginning to fill the sidewalks.

Shlomo leaned on the horn.

"That's quite all right, Shlomo." Mrs. Parkinson tapped their driver on the shoulder. "I'm sure we'll arrive at our destination soon enough."

Shlomo checked his rearview mirror with a grin and a wink for Emily.

"Oh dear." Her mother pointed out the window. "Another store boarded up. I wonder what is to become of this place when . . ."

Her voice trailed off, as if their thin bubble had finally burst. But how could it not? Everywhere, signs of the latest fighting stared them in the face. The burned-out shops. The sandbags piled in front of windows. The slogans scrawled on alley walls.

Emily turned her eyes away after reading the first one or two. "Perhaps this wasn't such a good idea," she whispered. "Perhaps we'd better go home."

"Nonsense, dear." But Mrs. Parkinson sounded none too convincing. "It was a fine idea. Shlomo, you just let us out here at Spinney's, and we'll be back in sixty minutes."

"Yes, Mrs. Parkinson." He nodded and pulled to the curb. "I'll be waiting over there, across the street."

He pointed to a couple of vacant parking spots in front of a pleasant three-story sandstone building. A battered gray panel van had just pulled into one of the adjacent spots, and a couple of men hopped out before disappearing quickly into an alley.

"One hour from now," repeated Shlomo. "Right over there."

Emily paused for a moment, gripping the car door just a second longer. Her mother had already strolled over to the front window of the store to glance at the dress display.

"Is that all right, Miss Emily?" Shlomo already had the car in gear, ready to drive. "Do you need more time than that?"

"No." Emily scratched her head and looked up to the morning sky. The day had started out clear, though rain clouds from the past week were gathering once more in the direction of Tel Aviv. Another storm? "No, that will be just fine."

Yet as she slammed the car door, something told her everything would *not* be fine.

Dov gazed up at the early-morning sky, looking for a trace of the clouds that had hung like dusty curtains over Jerusalem for the past week. All he could see were several gold-tinged cotton balls off to the northeast, hovering over the Old City walls, and then a few more in the direction of Tel Aviv. The sun rose fresh across the valley, its rays reaching westward toward Emily Parkinson's city, the "New" City.

New in name only. Because even Emily's part of Jerusalem held avenues of stately old brownstone two-story buildings, rows of sturdy-looking stone apartment buildings, and bustling streets full of Jewish shops. The New City—well, anything was new compared to the ancient walled city he now stared at, across the narrow but deep Hinnom Valley. The new and the old were as different as two cities could be.

Actually, the New City pleasantly reminded him of Warsaw, since it felt more European. If he could manage to avoid all the military roadblocks and checkpoints, it might be a good place to explore, a chance to escape the Parkinsons' cramped home for a while.

"Back in forty-five minutes," he whispered to the raven standing guard in the branches of an olive tree. "They won't even know I've been gone."

As he walked through the quiet olive grove along the ravine's edge, he wondered what kind of mess he'd gotten himself into. Rachel and Anthony he could understand, maybe. But how could people like them be related to Emily's father, a British army officer?

And then there was Tristan. Dov had learned that he sometimes helped a semi-secret Haganah radio station in the New City, somewhere off Ben Yehuda Street. Tristan was a friend of Anthony's from way back. They talked about radio things until late at night—transmitters, watts, relays . . .

It all seemed like a mixed-up puzzle, with pieces that didn't match. How he fit into it, Dov didn't know; all he really knew was he had to find Natan. And as crazy as it sounded, maybe these people could help him.

Dov juggled the questions as he picked up his pace down King George Avenue. Ahead and to the left, the New City of Jerusalem was coming to life for another day, shaking off the rumors of war. A delivery truck roared by in a cloud of smoke. A second-story window creaked open, and an older woman shook her small rug into the fresh morning air.

"How do you like this one?" Emily's mother tried on her third hat, turned from the back-room mirror, and smiled at her daughter. "Do you think it suits me?"

"Heavenly."

Emily couldn't remember seeing her mother smile so much, not in a long time. Was it the trip to Spinney's Department Store, or something else? Her mother cocked her head to the side and perched the rim of the hat just so. For just a moment all the ugliness of the latest fighting seemed far, far away—the riots, Arabs versus Jews, the shootings, the battles in the hills she read about in the newspaper. All the things her parents talked about in hushed whispers when her father came home with a dark expression in his eyes.

Emily's mother clowned with her hat, pulling it low over her eyes. Emily could almost forget everything and smile, too. But only for a moment.

If it takes going back to England to see her laugh again, thought Emily, *then I suppose it's worth it.*

Emily was just about to hand her mother another hat, a white one with baby's-breath netting and a pretty yellow bow, when the Thunder hit.

A distant, mighty *boom* shook Jerusalem like an angry clap of thunder.

Dov felt the explosion as much as he heard it. Nearby windows rattled in protest as the explosion echoed through the valleys around him. The woman above him dropped her rug in surprise, and it fluttered to the pavement. Others ran out into the street, calling to one another.

"What happened?"

"Did you hear that?"

"What was it?"

"A bomb!"

Just above the trees and between two three-story apartment buildings, Dov saw a thick black mushroom cloud of smoke rising. Moments later the sickly wail of a siren told him something was indeed wrong.

Without another thought, Dov started running toward the site of the explosion.

The clap of the explosion sounded right beside Emily, as if someone had blown up an enormous paper sack and popped it next to her head. She screamed and grabbed for her mother as the floor trembled in an earthquake unlike any she had known before. In the instant after the blast, she had but one thought:

Hold on to Mum!

A moment later the department store was filled with shattered glass, screams, and frightened sobs. Dark, dust-filled smoke billowed past piles of tumbled mannequins, jumbled dress racks, and shredded bedding. It seemed as if half the ceiling had caved in, though it was hard to tell in the dim light.

"Mummy!" Emily choked on the plaster dust and clutched her mother with all her strength.

"Oh dear," sobbed Mrs. Parkinson. "Whatever has happened?"

Together, they huddled behind what had once been the dressing rooms in the back of the store. Emily was afraid to move—all the full-length mirrors had slivered into a million wicked shards around them. By some grace of God, she could not feel the wetness of blood on herself or her mother, though she would have to wait until they were outside in the daylight to be sure. In any case, with every ragged breath she breathed a prayer of thanks that they had not been standing at the front of the store, as they had been just a few minutes earlier.

But then another thought gripped her, and she rose to her feet in horror.

"Shlomo!" she whispered. "Where's Shlomo?"

END OF THE WORLD

6

"We can't help Shlomo now, dear." Emily's mother held tightly to her.

"Is anyone back there?" yelled a man from the front of the store. Emily could barely make out his form through the haze and smoke.

She choked back her tears. "We're here!" She gripped her mother's hand and took one careful step. "We're alive!"

But what about Shlomo? Emily did her best to thread her way through the ruined store, but it was as if they had entered a new world—one she would never choose to visit. Before long, the screams of those caught in this nightmare were matched by the screams of sirens and shouts of rescuers. Emily struggled through the debris and wounded, making sure at each step that her mother stayed by her side.

A clerk from the store held a fashionable blue-striped scarf to her bloody forehead. Others were cut, too, but miraculously, most everyone looked as if they were on their feet. Some looked like ghosts, covered with fine white dust from the ceilings and walls. Others sobbed in fright.

"Shlomo . . ." Emily whispered. The glass front of the store had shattered and now carpeted the lobby in a dangerous, glittering layer. Her mother leaned on her for support as they tiptoed through the glass to finally peer outside into the smoking holocaust.

"Ohhhh . . ." Mrs. Parkinson's knees buckled, and Emily did her best to keep her mother from falling. "It's the end of the world."

Emily's stomach turned at what they saw, and she thought perhaps her mother was right. Maybe it *was* the end of the world. Certainly the end of *her* world. Only the fact that she still breathed told her otherwise.

The building straight across from them had partially collapsed, leaving only a story and a half where there had once been three. Most of the other nearby buildings were still standing, but only barely. Glass and brick, concrete and plaster had been thrown apart and mashed together again, until Emily wasn't quite sure what she was looking at. She thought she remembered an office building on the corner. But now smoke poured from gaping holes where there had once been windows, and papers floated to the ground like ghostly butterflies.

This can't be!

A portrait of a smiling baby gazed up at her from behind a broken glass frame; perhaps it had come tumbling down from an office worker's desk. A robin's-egg blue hat lay crushed beneath a pile of strangely twisted mannequins and a wreck of metal pipes. Even worse, the street's vehicles had been swept together in a maelstrom of fire and debris. Rubble covered most of the smoking, twisted black remains of several cars and delivery trucks, jumbled up with goodness knows what else. The charred pages of someone's ledger book came to rest at Emily's feet, revealing neat columns of handwritten red numbers for anyone to see.

But this would never add up. Emily turned her head to breathe, but the acrid smoke from a bonfire of blackened beams and cracked bricks followed them everywhere. She could not escape the sights, sounds, and stench of death.

"Oh, Lord," she prayed, "please let me wake up in my own bed, away from this nightmare."

But of course Emily knew that would not happen. Had she and her mother really been standing there on the busy sidewalk of Ben Yehuda Street only minutes before?

Emily could not force her mind to clear, could not make her arms and legs move to do anything to help. Again, she felt the terror of the bomb blast as it had pressed against them.

"Your father will be here soon." Emily's mother leaned against the outer wall, her tear-soaked face cradled in her hands.

But Major Parkinson would be too late to make this horror go away.

"Emily!" She jumped at the sound of someone calling her name.

No, it was not her father. Instead, Emily glanced up to see the grim face of Dov Zalinski as he stumbled over a pile of smoking debris.

"What are you doing here?" Emily did not want to start crying, not just then. But she could hold back the tears as easily as she could have stopped the blast. They just tumbled out.

"I heard the explosion, saw the . . ." Dov's flow of words stopped as he looked around at the bomb site. He had seen such things before, of course, during the war. He had made it through the destruction of Warsaw's Jewish ghetto and survived the Nazi-run munitions plant at Czestochowa, where he had been forced to work. And the death camp. Dachau.

But still, Dov felt sick at the sight before him. Where he supposed parents had been walking with their baby strollers, now the sidewalk was filled with pieces of broken buildings, broken cars, and . . . He shuddered to think.

"Our driver, Shlomo!" Emily sobbed. "He was out—"

"What?" Dov couldn't make out the words as another screaming ambulance pulled around the corner of Jaffa Road and two more men piled out.

Emily cupped her hands and leaned closer. "Shlomo! He was out here waiting in our car!"

"In your car?" Dov remembered the big American car he had ridden in weeks before, when Emily and her father had given him a ride. He scanned the street, but no car or truck within a quarter block could be driven away.

Emily pointed. "He said he would wait for us over there."

"Over there" was a pile of waist-high broken concrete and glass, covering a twisted metal shape that looked as if it might have once been a truck or a car. Dov took a step, then hesitated.

"What about your parents?"

Emily looked over her shoulder at a woman still standing on the sidewalk, her face buried in her hands. A blanket rested around her shoulders.

"Mother?"

The woman looked up, but her stare was as bleak and empty as the bombed-out storefronts around them. She said nothing.

"She'll be all right," Dov decided. "What about your driver?"

"Over here, I think." Quickly, she led the way to the wreckage.

Dozens of other rescuers had already started pulling people out of the debris, but not from this pile. No one seemed to notice or care, except for a wide-eyed British soldier who ran up to them.

"Stay back!" he ordered them. "It's too dangerous."

"Only if you're buried under this stuff," grunted Emily. She tugged at a piece of loose concrete and heaved it a few inches toward the soldier's feet.

He took one look at her set jaw and tear-stained cheeks, shrugged, and turned away.

"Help me with this." Dov wrestled one side of another piece of concrete; Emily grabbed the other. They dug together like desperate, starving dogs searching for a bone. Dov hoped for Emily's sake they would find more than that.

"Animals," mumbled Dov. "Animals did this."

They dug on in silence, looking for any sign of the Parkinsons' military car. Ten minutes later they had uncovered enough of a truck to be sure they were in the wrong place.

"Look at this!" Dov held up a piece of flat metal with red block writing on the side. *Egged Parcel Service.* At least *that* piece of metal was not *their* piece of metal.

Emily rested her hands on her knees and gasped for air. Her shoulders slumped.

But the grim search had only begun. Dov glanced back at the sidewalk to see that Emily's father had not yet arrived. Others had, though, and they wailed at the wreckage and shouted the names of loved ones: Nahman and Rebecca, Judah and Miriam . . .

And where was Shlomo? Dov remembered the friendly face of the big man behind the wheel of the Parkinsons' car. And he dug like the other would-be rescuers, pulling aside crumpled metal, kicking chunks of concrete to the side. They had moved away to another pile of rubble, farther down the street. That would be better—each step they took away from the center of the blast meant a step toward Shlomo's possible survival.

"Maybe he wasn't parked where you thought he was parked."

Emily shrugged and flipped a dirty wisp of hair away from her sweat-drenched forehead.

"I don't know," she admitted. "I don't know anything anymore."

"Emily!" a man called to her, and she turned to face her uniformed father.

"Oh, Daddy!" She rushed over to the sidewalk to jump into his arms.

Dov turned his face, inched away, and pretended not to notice. Several feet away, he was sure he heard a groan.

He yanked away a striped red-and-green awning to uncover an accordion of gray metal trimmed with chrome. Another car!

Dov was just about to turn for help when he heard the groan again. And this time, faint words.

"Please . . . help."

Dov thought he could tell where the voice came from. If he could just pull away one more piece of broken concrete, he could crawl down to where the driver might be. He leaned lower until he saw first the fingers, then a battered arm. A finger moved.

This man was alive!

"I'll get help!" Dov was about to back out, but the voice again called to him.

"No, wait. Please."

Dov leaned closer. What had happened to the other rescuers? It wasn't going to be easy getting this man out. An entire wall looked as if it had fallen on the car, crushing it to probably half its usual height.

"I'll be right back, mister," Dov told him. "Really, I—"

"No. Don't go. Please."

A finger brushed his hand, and Dov hesitated.

"Come closer."

Dov squirmed in on his stomach another several inches, until he looked straight into the face of Shlomo, Emily's driver. He felt a weak hand on his, pulsing with only the faintest hint of life.

"Are you . . . Mr. Shlomo?" Dov whispered. It was as if the world around them had faded away, and nothing else was real. The man studied Dov through puffed, squinty eyes.

"If I'm alive, you're Emily's friend," the man finally gasped. "Or if I'm dead, you're an angel."

"I'm no angel," Dov assured him. "But give me a minute, and we can get you out of here."

"No!" The fingers closed around Dov's hand. "Listen to me. I'm not going anywhere. God sent you to me before I go."

At the words, Dov felt a tear roll down his cheeks. Tears for a man he hardly knew.

"You're not going to die. We'll get you some help."

"No," murmured Shlomo, his lips hardly moving. He grimaced. "You're ma'apil, aren't you?"

What kind of question was that? Why did it matter to this man if Dov was an illegal immigrant to the Holy Land, a ma'apil? "Yes, sir, but—"

"Does Major Parkinson know where you come from?"

Dov was not sure where this was going.

"Maybe. Emily told him I helped her. But I don't think he's paid much attention to me."

"Good. Do . . . do you know any Haganah?"

Dov thought of Rachel and Anthony, who were probably wondering what had happened to their guest. They, of course, were Haganah. He still wasn't sure if he could trust them, but . . .

"Only Rachel and Anthony, but I don't think I should—"

The man's eyes snapped wide open. "Perfect. You were sent to me, boy. Now, quickly, before anyone else comes. My pocket. An envelope. Take it to them."

His eyes pleaded in a way Dov had never seen before. Dov nodded and reached across the man's chin, feeling for a shirt pocket. There! A bulky envelope.

"Take this . . . and give it to your Haganah friends. To them only, and no one else! Tell them it is from Shlomo . . . and they will understand."

"Uh, all right." Dov stuffed the bulging envelope into his shirt. "But now, let me find someone to help you."

"No one else must know, understand?" The man's words were so soft now, Dov had to lean his ear right next to his face to hear. "Not Emily, and especially not Major Parkinson."

His voice trailed off, and his fingers slid down Dov's arm and dropped away. Dov leaned even closer, close enough to touch the man's nose with his cheek. And his own blood went cold when he could not feel even the softest breath of life.

"Help!" Dov squirmed out backward, away from the wrecked Plymouth and began shouting at the top of his lungs. "We need some help over here!"

AMONG THE RUINS

Emily wondered if the nightmare would ever end. When a group of soldiers finally pulled Shlomo's body from their flattened car, her mother collapsed into her father's arms. The sound of another siren made Emily want to scream. But there was nowhere to hide from the scene except perhaps home under the covers, in her own bed.

"Please can we go home now, Daddy?"

Her father turned from talking to a rescue worker to her and her mother, pain in his eyes. By that time dozens of men swarmed over the wreckage. Fire fighters doused the last of the fires—smoldering piles of splintered floorboards, massive beams, cardboard crates, women's dresses. Even two hours after the first blast, a pall of black smoke still hung over the downtown, as if it were in mourning. Was there anything else the major could do here? He held up his hand for Emily to wait a moment and flagged down one of the rescuers.

"Is everyone accounted for in the British Foreign Service office up there?" he asked. When the young man gave him a blank stare, Major Parkinson grabbed him by the collar and pointed toward a row of shattered third-floor windows.

"Up there, man! The . . . oh, never mind. Not many people were supposed to know the office was there. From the looks of this mess, I suppose Jewish terrorists did, though."

The young man looked as if he finally understood. "I heard everyone got out of the building all right, sir. A few people down on the street, though, they . . ."

Major Parkinson let go of the man's shirt, dusted off his hands, and looked briefly at the ground.

"Right. Terribly sorry, chap, it's just that I had friends working there. Reminded me of another time. I didn't mean to—"

"Of course, sir."

The young man nodded and hurried away, leaving them alone.

"This is my fault," Major Parkinson mumbled.

"Daddy?" Emily stepped over to her father, holding on to him so he wouldn't run off again.

"My fault for not rounding up more of those Jewish terrorists."

That would be the *Irgun*, the radical splinter group that considered the Haganah too soft. But would they really have done something as dreadful as this? Emily couldn't be sure. Perhaps her father was only guessing. She remembered him once saying *Arab* terrorists would strike. But what good would it do to remind him of that now?

"Oh, Daddy, it's not your fault. You've done the best you could."

"Sometimes that's just not good enough, princess."

"That's not what you tell *me*."

"Eh, what?" His shoulders sagged, and his hard expression cracked.

"You tell me to do my best and leave the rest up to God. Isn't that so?"

"I suppose you're right, Emily. I just wish you and your mother hadn't been here. And Shlomo."

"I wish, too, Daddy."

They were both silent for a minute; then the major asked, "What about your friend? What happened to him?"

"You mean Dov." Emily wiped her eyes and gazed around. Dov had disappeared in the confusion of the last half hour.

"Perhaps he should come home with us," her father went on. "He was the first one to find Shlomo's . . . er, Shlomo. I'd like to thank him myself."

"I haven't seen him for a while." Emily sighed.

"You don't know where he is?"

Emily shook her head, unable to speak, unable to move. Shlomo was dead, and there was nothing she could do to change that. Her father had to help her to a military car parked on the edge of the bombed-out street.

She needed to go home.

Dov watched Emily and her parents from around the corner, waiting until they left. Searchers and soldiers still surrounded and sifted what was left of the blast scene. He held up his hands in front of his face. They shook.

What now? He shuffled through the glass, his stomach empty, his body trembling, his mind blank. He had not felt so numb since Dachau. Everything that had happened to him in the last two hours was a blur, from the time he first heard the bomb, to finding Emily and her mother, to digging through the ruins, to finding the crushed car.

Still in a daze, he wandered through an alley to an open doorway behind the main blast, to part of a building that had been somewhat spared. Its door hung on a single hinge and the windows were gone. Inside, he could see a portion of the ceiling had caved in, leaving a mess of plaster and splintered boards over most of the floor. He could see daylight not just through the windows, but through the gaping high ceilings, as well. No one would be living in this building for a while.

"Hello?" Dov felt like an intruder, but if someone was hurt inside, he might be needed. "Is anyone here?"

No one answered, so he slowly stepped inside. A small entry held a simple table and three mismatched hard wooden chairs. A fallen bookcase had dumped books all over the floor—mostly travel and history books. But what really caught Dov's eye was the closet door that had been *behind* the bookcase.

"What's this?" He stooped through the opening to enter a mostly dark room, lit only by the gray afternoon sunlight trickling through the ceiling.

"Is anyone in here?"

Obviously not. Or at least, no one answered.

But once his eyes got used to the shadows, Dov could see this was no ordinary closet. Otherwise, why the secret door? Against the near wall, three square black metal cabinets still stood one on top of the other. Dials and switches lined the face of each. And against the far side of the tiny room, a school desk was covered with still more metal cabinets, as well as a large radio-style microphone on a stand.

A radio broadcast station?

Dov could only guess. He'd never seen this kind of equipment close up. It wouldn't hurt to spin the dial a little, would it? But a sound from behind him made him freeze.

"Look at this mess, Avi." Someone stepped in through the broken alley door.

Dov heard the deep Hebrew voice before he saw the shadows fall across the doorway behind him. Without a sound he ducked below the desk. It wasn't hard to hide in the dark. Two pairs of shoes crunched into the small room.

"Just look at it."

"I'm looking, Eliahu. Just give my eyes a minute."

"You're the technical expert. Can we salvage anything?"

By that time Dov could almost smell the men's breath. "I think it might still work, if we just had some power."

"Sure, but what about the building? Next time it rains— and that's probably tonight—we can stand in here with umbrellas, eh? Now, *that* would be good for the equipment. And what about our announcer?"

"You heard them say he'll live."

"A good thing. In the meantime the Haganah has no voice—no radio station, no power, no announcers, nothing. And nowhere to go, either."

What had the man said? The Haganah?

"Ah, we'll find somewhere to go," said Avi. "Let me get a look at this wiring."

Dov held his breath, glad the lights weren't working. But a moment later he heard the scratching of a cigarette lighter, and then the room was filled with a feeble gold light as the two young men studied their equipment. Dov tried to pull his arm in, back into the shadows, but that turned out to be a mistake. One man noticed the little movement and jumped as if he had just discovered a rat.

"Hey!" he yelped and spun to face Dov, who had nowhere to go. "What's this? *Who's* this?"

He held the lighter so close to Dov's face, he might have singed Dov's eyebrows.

"I was just . . . looking." Dov blinked in the light. "Checking to see if anybody needed help."

"Help?" The men glanced at each other and shook their heads. "Do we look as if we need help?"

"What do you think, Eliahu?" Avi asked his round-faced, bearded friend as they studied Dov. Avi was slight and dark-haired, with a long neck and a longer nose.

"No one needs help here, kid," decided Eliahu. He backed up and pointed toward the door with his thumb. "Out."

Fine with me. Dov scrambled to his feet and headed straight for the door. But a thought stopped him as he was about to step out into the alley. He looked back over his shoulder as raindrops began to fall.

"I know where you might be able to set up your station," he told them.

Emily was past tears as she and her parents ate that night. Their cook, Wardi, said nothing, either, as she brought a custard dessert and cleared plates. Only the wall clock dared break the silence.

"We should never have gone there," Emily finally mumbled.

Her father tossed his napkin on a plate. "You needn't go blaming yourself. It's no use at all. We've been over it now a hundred times. It was no one's fault."

Emily raised her eyebrows.

"I mean," he corrected himself, "no one here. Now, the Jewish terrorists, that's another thing. They seem to have no qualms about killing one of their own."

For a moment a picture flashed into Emily's mind: the old gray panel van parking across the street from Spinney's Department Store, and the two men hurrying away into the alley. Could it have been?

"But, Daddy, what if it *wasn't* Jewish terrorists? What if it was someone else?"

"I don't think so." As he rubbed his temples, Emily thought he looked older than ever before. "I've been getting closer and closer to an Irgun group that might be responsible. If I could just catch up with them before E-Day . . ."

E-Day. Evacuation Day for the British, just a month away. Emily heard the word all the time now.

"E-Day . . ." Emily whispered and glanced at her mother. Mrs. Parkinson had a faraway look in her eyes and didn't seem to be paying attention to what they were saying.

Emily's father went on about the Irgun. "They're animals, I tell you. Rob their own mothers, if you give them a chance. You should know that as well as anyone, after what they did to you. If you hadn't escaped and been rescued . . . Animals . . ."

Emily remembered Dov's words as they were digging through the rubble.

"Sounds like something Dov said," she whispered.

"What's that?"

"Oh nothing, Daddy. Dov just said something like that, too."

"I see." He paused, rubbing his chin. "We never did find him, did we? Did he just run off?"

Emily nodded, wishing she hadn't brought it up.

"Emily, how well do you know this Dov fellow? You never really told me the entire story of your meeting. Just Dov, is that right? Doesn't he have a surname?"

Emily hesitated, wondering how much she should tell her father. Of course he meant well, and she trusted him to the end. But perhaps it wouldn't sound good, the part about Dov coming here on a ship of illegal immigrants, and all. No, that wouldn't sound good at all. Better not to say anything that might put Dov in danger.

"His name is Dov Zalinski," she said. "And—"

"Wait a minute." He pointed his custard spoon at her. "Zalinski, you say?"

Emily nodded.

"Why didn't you tell me that before?"

"I . . ." Emily wasn't sure how to explain. "I didn't think it mattered."

"All right, then, go on. Dov Zalinski."

"Well, yes. He can be a bit of a hothead at times, but . . ."

She tried to tell her father more about her friend, but he rubbed his chin and seemed to think of something else.

"Wait just a minute." He held up his finger and excused himself from the table. "I'll be right back."

Mrs. Parkinson didn't seem to notice his departure. She stared at the wall clock and slowly scraped the bottom of her bowl of custard.

The major returned a minute later with a manila file in hand.

"I *knew* I'd heard that name before!" He jabbed his finger at a report as he sat back down. "Zalinski. Says here in my report that Natan Zalinski recently changed his name to Natan Israeli. How many Zalinskis do you think there are in Palestine? Dozens? A handful? I'd be willing to bet there's some connection."

Emily looked at her bowl and pushed at a clump of errant

custard. She could feel a horrible headache coming on, all on account of Dov. "They're brothers."

"Brothers?" His voice raised a notch.

"Yes, but I don't think Dov knows where Natan is. He's been looking for him."

"Perhaps . . . not yet."

Emily shifted in her chair. What exactly did *that* mean?

Her father went on. "This Natan Zalinski—er, Israeli—if he's who I think he is, he's one of the Irgun's top bomb experts. I'd be willing to wager he had something to do with setting the one that killed Shlomo."

Emily shivered at the thought.

"And I'm going to find him."

Suddenly Emily was afraid her father might do just that.

SHLOMO'S GIFT

8

"One thing is sure." Avi led the way through the dark Jerusalem streets, balancing a transmitter on his shoulder. "I would never have believed this street kid if he hadn't mentioned that he knew Tristan."

"What's that?" Dov's ears were ringing, and it was growing worse. His head ached, and his arms were sore from three trips schlepping boxes of heavy radio equipment from the bombed-out building to the Parkinsons' place in Yemin Moshe.

"I said," Avi repeated himself, "it's a good thing about you knowing Tristan."

"Oh yeah, we've . . . er, met."

"No kidding." Avi wasn't slowing down for anyone, but Dov wasn't quite sure they were doing the right thing, not after seeing the surprised look on Anthony's face when they'd first showed up at his door.

"Are you sure they're going to let us set up in their back room?" Eliahu had the same question as Dov. "Just like that?"

"He said yes, didn't he?" Avi grunted.

"Sort of." Eliahu didn't sound convinced. "Probably only

because he saw how desperate we are."

"You have any better ideas? Besides, it's only for a few weeks, until we find some money to rent a safer place."

Money. Dov patted his shirt pocket one more time just to be sure it was still there. He would give the envelope to Rachel Parkinson and no one else. For now, it was a good thing these two men didn't know, as Dov did, that it was stuffed with English pounds. If they found out, they might try to take it away from him.

"Wait a minute." When he stopped to catch his breath, the world around him seemed to swim in circles.

"Hold up, Avi," huffed Eliahu. He looked around the dark street for passersby.

After a few moments Dov shouldered his load again, a box stuffed full of wires and microphones. It wasn't quite as heavy as the other crates he'd carried, but for some reason, his knees turned to rubber and his legs to noodles. The damp pavement looped around and came up to meet him.

"Hey, kid!" Avi's voice sounded far away. "What's wrong?"

Never mind the evening dark. Everything went completely black.

Emily backed her chair away from the dining-room table. This was definitely *not* one of their friendly father-daughter discussions, and her headache was getting worse. But her father wore his most serious military expression as he leaned forward in his spot at the head of the table. He was not going to stop digging for more information about Dov Zalinski and his brother, Natan.

"I don't believe Dov has seen his brother since he was little," she whispered. "He's been looking for him, but—"

"This is perfect!" Major Parkinson slammed his hand down on the table. "Simply perfect. Don't you see? If you meet Dov again, you must ask him if he's made contact with his brother, find out—"

Emily gasped. "You want *me* to be a spy?"

Her father shook his head. "Oh no, no—nothing like that. All you have to do is find out where the brother is staying, assuming your friend knows where his own brother is."

"I told you he doesn't. He's looking."

Her father took her hands in his. "Believe me, princess, I would never ask you to do something I thought was at all dangerous. This opportunity is simply too good to pass up."

A spoon clattered to the table, and they both turned to see Emily's mother glaring at them.

"You . . . will . . . not." She took a deep breath, as if each word were painful. "You will not . . . *use* Emily in this way!"

Major Parkinson started to say something, then changed his mind. He reached over and touched his wife's hand, but she pulled away.

"How can you even *think* of it after what just . . . what just . . ." Her words dissolved in a stream of tears.

"I'm sorry, dear. I should not have mentioned it just now. We're all still in shock, I fear. We cared for Shlomo a great deal."

Emily closed her eyes and agreed. Was this what shock felt like?

"Alan, this is about more than shock," cried Emily's mother. "This is an obsession! First it's the illegal radio station. Now it's these terrorists. Or is it all the same thing?"

Major Parkinson looked ready to apologize, but he wasn't quite changing his mind. "All I'm saying, dear, is that if Emily happens to meet Dov again before I do, she should simply ask a few general questions. Perhaps we can get to the bottom of things more quickly this way. That is all right, Emily, is it not?"

Emily struggled to open her eyes, and her temples were now throbbing. What could she say that would satisfy her father?

"I think Dov may be staying with Bin-Jazzi," Emily finally whispered and crossed her arms. She remembered what Dov had told her at Aunt Rachel's. "That shopkeeper who was in the hospital. Street of the Chain."

"Bin-Jazzi. Right." The major nodded and jotted something down in the margin of his paper, then looked up with a question on his face. "Street of the Chain. That's in the, er, Muslim Quarter, isn't it?"

Wardi entered the room to take out more dishes.

Emily nodded. "May I be excused, please?"

"Of course you may, dear," answered her mother.

The only thing Emily wanted to do now was crawl under the covers of her bed, as soon as possible. She headed for the door without another word.

She didn't tell her father about seeing Dov at Aunt Rachel's house.

It simply wouldn't do to get Aunt Rachel in trouble, she reminded herself. *And besides, Daddy will find out for himself sooner or later.*

Probably sooner.

The next time Dov opened his eyes, it was still dark. He wasn't sure what woke him. But at least the world wasn't twirling anymore.

"Where am I?" he asked. He lay on a sofa decked out with clean sheets and blankets, but nothing looked familiar. Not the little prints of famous Dutch paintings on the walls. Not the flowers on the table beside him. He propped himself up on his elbow to hear the muffled sound of someone talking in the next room.

"In other news," said a man from the other side of a half-closed door, "four Jews and two Arabs were killed near Jaffa Tuesday during a series of skirmishes near Abu Kebir on the Jaffa-Jerusalem Road. Authorities say . . ."

Oh yes. But Rachel and Anthony Parkinson's home was not quite how he remembered it from the night before. He slipped off the sofa and padded over to see what was happening in the other room.

"Several demonstrations also took place in the Jaffa region, including one with four hundred schoolboys parading with banners and slogans."

It looked for all the world as if the Haganah radio station had taken up permanent residence at Number 3 Malki Street. The bed in the second bedroom had been shoved off to the side, while a folding card table tottered under the weight of radio transmitters—the same ones he had helped bring from the bombed-out building. Avi crouched on his knees behind one, poking at a couple of wires with a screwdriver. Anthony's friend Tristan was there, too, looking over his shoulder and telling Avi what to do. Avi ignored the other man, while Anthony sat in front of a microphone, reading aloud.

"Oh, there you are, Dov." Rachel came from the kitchen with an armful of clean towels. "Feeling better?"

"Shh!" Avi looked up and warned them with a finger to his lips.

"Whoops, sorry." She retreated to the living room and lowered her voice. "I guess I'm not used to having a radio station in my home."

"Are they really broadcasting already?" Dov whispered. He wanted to watch some more.

Rachel nodded. "They didn't want to waste any time, so while you were sleeping they set up in the other bedroom. But you, my friend—do you know you slept on that couch fourteen hours straight?"

"Fourteen?" Dov peeked in again at the buzz of activity in Anthony and Rachel's bedroom. His back was stiff.

"I think you were in shock or something. Avi and Eliahu said you were acting strangely, like you were dizzy. You were talking in your sleep, too."

"What did I say?"

"Not much we could understand, except that you wanted to see Natan." She put down her towels on the end of the sofa. "And we're going to call a doctor if you have any more fainting spells."

"I was just tired."

"Maybe you were. But listen, maybe we should make something clear, okay?"

Dov crossed his arms.

"We'd love to have you stay here with us for a while. The cat won't bother you; he's outside all the time. And Anthony and I have prayed about it."

"Prayed?"

"Yes, prayed." She smiled, and the idea didn't seem so strange to Dov.

"We both want to help. Maybe you don't understand, but our ministry is here. Doing this sort of thing is how we serve the Lord."

She pointed at the radio setup. Dov still wasn't sure he understood. But he nodded and let her continue.

"And I want you to know we're glad you suggested the radio

boys come here, even though I'm sure Anthony and I looked a bit shocked last night when you showed up at the door with all that equipment."

"I was hoping . . ."

"It's fine. Really it is. They would never have thought to ask us. Avi said you practically dragged them here."

"Well . . ."

"Like I said, we're glad to have the radio equipment for a couple of weeks, until they get their roof fixed or find another space. Anthony's so involved that he's already helping out with the announcing, can you believe it? I think it's a terrible idea, but they said his voice is perfect for that sort of thing, and it's just temporary."

"But what about Emily's father?"

"We talked about that." She nodded seriously. "Anthony thinks we'll be safe with the equipment in the bedroom, especially since Alan never comes to visit anymore. Of course, there's a danger he might hear one of the broadcasts, but—"

"But?"

"Well," she waved her hand toward the bedroom studio. "I have a feeling we're going to have to be very quiet for the next few weeks. The Haganah isn't on the air twenty-four hours a day, but we're not going to be able to make much noise for a while."

"I don't shout too loudly in my sleep."

"That's the first joke I've heard from you." Rachel looked at him with a sideways glance. "That *was* a joke, right?"

Dov looked at the floor.

"Oh." She held up her finger, as if remembering something. "I also wanted to tell you that having the radio station here gives you a way to help, ah, earn your bed and keep. We'll need you to run messages, do errands—that sort of thing. Avi and Eliahu could use the help. Tristan's here sometimes, but you know what he's like."

"Right." Dov winced at the memory of the man's boots. "I can help. But I need time to find my brother, too. He's out there somewhere."

"I assume he's illegal, like you?"

"No." Dov felt his face flush. "Emily saw his name in the newspaper on some kind of list. He changed his name from Natan Zalinski to Natan Israeli."

"Hmm. I'm not sure I've heard that name before. I'll ask Anthony."

"So you'll help me find him?"

"Hold your horses! We'll help as much as we can, but I can't say how much. We do know a few people. We'll ask around."

Dov sighed with relief.

"Oh, one more thing."

"Yes?"

"Next time you run off to an explosion, would you do me a favor and tell me where you're going? I know I'm not your mother, but if you're going to be staying with us . . ."

Dov paused for a moment. The thought had never crossed his mind to tell anyone where he was going. Who cared where he went? But—

"Uh . . . sure. If that's what you want."

"And we usually eat lunch around noon, which is a half hour from now. For you it's going to be breakfast; you're all confused! But you're going to have to do some serious washing up before you sit down to eat."

Dov tried not to grin. What had she said about not being his mother? He grabbed one of her towels and started to slip quietly to the bathroom. But then he remembered the envelope, and he glanced back at the couch.

The thought crossed Dov's mind—just for a second—that he could probably find a way to spend so much money. Maybe he could even share it with Mr. Bin-Jazzi. The Arab shopkeeper could certainly use the money. For a second it seemed like a good thing to do.

But only for a second. Because when he glanced back at the envelope next to the sofa, all he could remember was Shlomo's wish. What had he said?

"Give it to your Haganah friends."

So what else could he do? A dying man had trusted him with a small fortune. The money wouldn't help him find Natan anyway. What else did he really care about?

"That envelope there is for you and Anthony. I don't know what you Haganah do with so much money, but it's for you."

Rachel raised her eyebrows and walked over to pick up the envelope.

"It's from Shlomo," Dov added. "He said you would un-derstand."

"Shlomo Yassky." Tears filled her eyes. "I heard."

"You knew him?" Dov had never before heard the man's last name.

"Yeah." She paused. "I suppose it won't hurt to tell you now. He, ah, worked for the Haganah, raising money. Maybe this will keep the station going."

"But—"

"But right under the nose of Major Alan Parkinson? Yes, it's true." Rachel gave a small smile. "On the one hand was Shlomo, faithful driver for the British. And on the other, Shlomo, secret fund-raiser for the Haganah freedom fighters. It didn't hurt that his job gave him a reason to have contact with Anthony and me."

"A double life."

Aunt Rachel nodded. "Shlomo found people who wanted to help. Even a few British gave money, though you probably know that many of them don't appreciate what we're doing. People need to hear the truth, though."

"I know."

As Dov stared at the secret radio station in the next room, he realized Shlomo wasn't the only one with a double life, a dangerous secret.

Now Dov had one, too.

THE SPY

9

"Oh. Terribly sorry."

Emily turned from the den's French doors, back toward the hallway. As far as she knew, her parents didn't often kiss—and never in public.

"It's all right, Emily," her father called after her. "Come back here, please."

By the time Emily returned to the den, her parents were sitting together on the sofa, still holding hands. She hovered by the door.

"Sit down, Emily. Your father has some good news for us. Wonderful news." Her mother offered a weak smile, the first Emily had seen in the three days since Shlomo's death.

But Emily didn't want to think about that now.

Her father cleared his throat. "You know I had hoped to keep us together until these difficulties were behind us. Your mother and I thought it important not to split up the family." He paused to look her in the eye. "But things have gotten out of hand. You know that, don't you?"

Emily squeezed her eyes shut and nodded. If explosions and

riots and mobs were out of hand, then yes, her father was right.

"So I've arranged to place you and your mother on a Norwegian steamer leaving Haifa this Friday."

The words echoed through the room. So this was it.

Major Parkinson went on. "It's just too dangerous for you to remain here any longer. And nothing matters but keeping you two safe."

Emily studied her mother's tear-streaked cheeks, her flushed face. A week ago, Emily might have stormed out of the room at the news. Now all her fight had withered, and she knew it.

"What about keeping *you* safe?" she croaked.

"I need to stay here until the last of the troops depart next month. Perhaps even a few days after that. We need to find those Irgun terrorists and close down that Haganah radio station. But you can be sure I'll join you at home just as soon as I'm free to go."

There was that empty word again.

Home.

It meant nothing to Emily. Not anymore. Not since she'd lost the only home she'd loved.

"You should know I had to pull some strings to get you the berths." He sounded proud of himself. "But it's all arranged. Flights . . . they were simply impossible."

So they would be separated after all. Emily and her mother cried for a time, holding on to each other and Mr. Parkinson. But in the end there was nothing to do but dry their eyes.

Julian shuffled up and licked the salty tears from the back of Emily's hand.

"Well, boy," she whispered. "Back where you came from, eh?"

"Uh, Emily." The good-news look on her father's face drained away. "There's something else I have to tell you."

Emily's heart fell to the floor. How could it get any worse than this?

"Julian isn't going."

"What?" Emily couldn't believe it. She must have heard her father wrong. Even Mrs. Parkinson stared at her husband as if he were playing a cruel joke. But they all knew better.

"I . . . I wanted to, Emily, you must believe me. But you know he's old, and he's sick, and the veterinarian says he simply can't make the trip. And even if he could, no one would ship him—not a Great Dane."

"We could keep him in our room." Emily's mind raced. "On the ship." There had to be a way.

But her father only shook his head. "I asked, dear. I nearly begged. But I could get tickets only for you, your mother, and that tutor of yours."

Perhaps Julian could use the third ticket? Emily didn't dare suggest what she was thinking as her father continued.

"I don't even know if we're going to be able to ship many of our things back to England. At the moment, every ship, every berth, every airplane is spoken for."

"But—"

"You must face the facts, dear. The old chap is at the end of his days. Ten years old. Older than you, actually, in dog years."

"I don't care about dog years," Emily sobbed. Her whole life she had grown up with Julian. He'd been her playmate when she was young. She couldn't remember a meal when he hadn't been right at her feet, ready for a handout. And what was a day without a walk with Julian?

"I'm so sorry, Emily." Her father stepped over and put his arm around her. "I know what the old boy has meant to you.

But he's not been well lately. You know that. Perhaps it's for the best."

"For the best?" That was too much. She ran from the room, pulling Julian behind her.

Half a block, turn around. Half a block, turn around. Julian was getting used to the routine now, as Emily pulled her big Great Dane back and forth in front of her home in the comfortable Rehavia District.

"To the corner and no farther," her mother had warned. And so in the early evening light, Emily paced back and forth in front of their home, like a guard and her guard dog. A few lights had already come on, mostly hidden by shutters and drapes. No one sat outside and talked to their neighbors, the way they used to. Even the wonderfully warm April weather didn't help matters, and Emily was pretty sure the people in these houses would be locked inside even if the weather were sweltering in mid-July.

"Sorry we can't go walking the way we used to." She leaned down and patted her old dog. Ten years old. That would be . . . she multiplied ten by seven . . . seventy in dog years. Did he look that old? "You must be getting frightfully bored of the same back and forth."

But Julian didn't seem to mind. He wagged his tail and sniffed the stone wall by the next-door neighbor's house, then shuffled slowly with her to the end of the block. Emily paused and looked before turning. A pebble hit her in the ankle, just above her rolled-down sock.

"Ow!" she mumbled and bent over to inspect her foot.

She looked around. They were the only walkers on the

street. Another pebble nicked her ear.

"Hey!"

Julian growled at the gardenia bushes on the corner, covered in creamy white blossoms. The hair on the back of Emily's neck stood up, as well. She yanked Julian's collar and backed away.

"Let's go home," she whispered, but then she saw a nose emerge from behind the flowering bush, followed by the rest of a boy's face.

"You!" she gasped.

"Me," Dov replied.

"Were you spying on me?" *That's a switch*, she thought. *I'm supposed to be spying on him.*

"I wouldn't have thrown a pebble at you if I were spying," Dov snapped back.

"You know what I mean."

"I have never known what you mean. I was just waiting for you here." He looked at her, and his eyes grew serious. "You look like you've been crying."

Emily ignored his last comment and looked around to see if anyone saw them. She could just walk away if anyone did and pretend she never saw Dov. And if he was going to speak to her the way he was, perhaps that's what she would do anyway.

"I knew you walked Julian every night." His answer seemed logical. "But I knew you couldn't go far. So I hid here and waited for you to come back."

"Well, if anyone sees you, he's going to call the police." Emily frowned. "Better if you'd just sit on the curb like a normal person."

"Speaking of normal people, I wonder what they'll think of you when they see you talking to a bush? Maybe you're practicing for the part of Moses?"

He giggled.

Emily didn't think it one bit funny. "Well then," she snapped, "you just get out of there this instant. Otherwise, I'll turn around and go home."

"No, wait. I came, ah . . . that is, I just wanted to check on you. See if you're all right."

Emily was about to snap back that she was just fine, thank you, when she stopped short. Had he ever worried about anyone else in his life? Anyone, aside from his family?

"I'm all right," she finally admitted. "Considering everything that's happened, I'd say that was quite good."

Dov didn't agree or disagree as he emerged from the bush to face her dog. She guessed Julian would probably take off into the sky, hind end first, if he wagged his propellor tail any harder.

"Here, boy." Dov scratched her dog behind the ears until Julian sat down, leaned his head to the side, kicked with his hind leg, and sighed.

"You're pretty good at that," she told Dov.

He grinned. "I've always wanted a dog."

"I've always had one." Emily bit her lip. She hadn't meant it the way it sounded.

Dov didn't seem to notice. "I'm really sorry about your—I mean, about Shlomo."

Emily nodded and wiped away a tear. Had he come to her neighborhood to remind her, to make it hurt all over again?

"Julian really likes you." She changed the subject.

"I guess so." Dov didn't look up. "Did I tell you I'm going to be working some?"

"Oh really? Did my aunt Rachel find something for you?"

"Yes. They're letting me sleep on a couch in the front room, too."

"So you're not staying in the Old City anymore?"

It was an innocent question, until she realized that was what her father wanted her to ask. Find out where he lives. Find out about his brother. Be a spy.

He shook his head. "It's hard to get in and out of the Old City. Sometimes impossible."

She knew that. Everyone knew.

"And what about your brother? Have you found him yet?"

Dov didn't look up or answer, just shook his head and scratched Julian.

"Listen, Dov—how much do you actually know about your brother?"

He looked up at her as if she had just slapped him on the cheek.

"How much do I *need* to know? He's my brother. My only family. Isn't that enough?"

So he doesn't know. Emily argued with herself, wondering what good it would do to tell him what her father had told her. *Your brother's a terrorist, Dov. He's a bad person. He blows up things.* Is that what she should say?

But Dov must have mistook her expression.

"You don't understand," he told her, turning away. "He's all I have, so I *have* to find him. You have *your* family, your home."

"What home?" She stomped her foot. Now it was her turn to get mad. "This *used* to be my home, but not anymore. Your people are taking it away from us!"

Again, Dov said nothing. Julian's tail thunked the sidewalk as Dov stroked his head.

Why had she said a silly thing like that?

"I'm sorry." She took a deep breath. "I wasn't going to tell you, but my mother and I are leaving in five days."

Dov's eyes widened for a moment, but he didn't answer right away.

"Did you hear me?"

"Yes. So not a month from now?"

"No. My father found passage for us on some kind of steamer."

"Really? Why aren't you going to fly in an airplane? I thought all British traveled in airplanes now."

"Not this one." She shrugged her shoulders. "Daddy said all flights are booked for weeks. And the worst part is, I . . . I can't take Julian."

He looked down at the dog, who licked him on the cheek.

"So what are you going to do with him?"

"Well, he likes you. How about . . ."

She had to say it. If not now, when?

"How about if you take care of him?"

Dov looked from Emily to Julian and back again.

"Me?" he asked. "Are you sure?"

"Yes, you. And you'd better say yes before I change my mind, Dov Zalinski. Otherwise, I'm afraid my father will just have him put away. Put . . . down. He says he's old and won't live much longer anyway."

"Well . . ." He scratched Julian behind one ear, then the other. "Sure. Whenever you want."

Part of Emily breathed a sigh of relief. Another part of her was ready to punch Dov in the jaw for saying yes so quickly. Before she had a chance to see which part would win, Emily turned and gave Julian's leash a shake.

"It's all settled, then," she told him, biting her lip to keep from crying. "You can come pick him up before we leave on the sixteenth. That's Friday. I'll give you his leash and collar, and his bowl, and he has a blanket he prefers to sleep on. I'll tell you what he likes to eat, and all that."

"I'll come here again," he answered. "Thursday night?"

"If you like." She took a couple of steps away.

"As long as your father isn't here. I don't think he likes me."

Emily didn't know how to answer. She kept walking, then stopped.

"Dov?"

"Yes?"

"About your brother again . . . I might, I might have heard something."

"What?" He spun around, eyes blazing.

She held up her hand. "No, I mean . . . I don't know anything for certain. All I heard is that he might be . . . with a group. That's all."

"What kind of group?"

Emily's mind raced. Should she tell him what she knew? Maybe it wasn't true after all. Who knew, really?

"It's not certain, but there's a chance he's with a group like the . . . perhaps the . . . Irgun."

His dark eyes narrowed, and he opened his mouth to say something but didn't. He must have known she couldn't tell him more, even if she had known anything else.

"Thanks," he mumbled and turned away. "Thanks."

"Thursday night?" She led Julian up the front steps to her door.

But there was no response. Dov was already sprinting down the street.

WAR
CORRESPONDENT

10

"Emily?" Major Parkinson poked his head into the kitchen.

"Yes, Daddy?" Emily looked up from one of the silver drawers, still trying to figure out which utensils to use for dinner. Two forks, a knife, and a spoon. Where did Wardi keep it all?

"You're a good sport to help like this, since Wardi left us." He smiled and rested a briefcase under his shoulder. "It's only until you leave for home, of course."

Emily nodded and held up a fork. She didn't want to talk about their cook's sudden decision to depart, supposedly to care for a sick mother in Beirut. Everybody was leaving, including her.

"Mum says dinner in less than an hour."

"Don't worry, I shall be ready. But I have been wondering, er, if you've heard anything else from Dov Zalinski. Has he mentioned anything about his brother?"

Emily's mouth went dry. She had gone from just plain Emily, to Emily the maid, to Emily the spy.

"We're closing in on him, mind you." Her father nearly grinned, he seemed so proud. "Some of my fellows have already spoken with that Bin-Jazzi fellow."

"What did he say?"

"Oh." The major cleared his throat. "Nothing just yet, but I think we'll learn something quite soon. I just thought perhaps you could . . . you know."

"Yes, sir." Emily turned back to sorting silverware. She could feel a headache coming on.

Dov wasn't sure what time it was when he heard the muffled ring of the telephone from Anthony and Rachel's room. He hadn't slept much. He lay quietly on his couch, wrapped in his blanket like a caterpillar in a cocoon, listening to the low murmur of voices.

At first it was all Anthony, and though Dov could not make out the words, there was an edge of excitement to his voice. Why would someone ring them in the middle of the night, unless something terrible had happened?

When Rachel's voice came through the wall, though, there was no mistaking her meaning.

"You will *not* leave me like this!"

More murmuring from Anthony.

"No, you don't need to," came Rachel once again. "You've been reporting the news just fine from right here this past week. This neighborhood is dangerous enough without you running off to a battle."

The murmur grew a little louder.

"This has nothing to do with my trusting *Yeshua*. I just don't want to be a widow, Anthony Parkinson. Do you hear me?"

Dov could hear her just fine, especially when Anthony quietly pushed their bedroom door open. Now he could hear both sides of the debate.

"People need to know what's really happening out there, dear. I'll be perfectly safe."

Dov cracked open one eye but didn't move as Anthony went on about "a battle for Kolonia." He sounded almost like a history professor.

One—Kolonia, the Arab town overlooking the highway to Jerusalem, was being used as a base for Arab attackers, he said. Two—no supplies could reach Jerusalem without making it past Kolonia. And three—Jewish forces wanted to retake that high ground. The Haganah would be there, Anthony explained, and perhaps also some men from the Irgun.

At that, Dov nearly fell off the couch. The Irgun? After what Emily had told him . . .

"I don't care about their battle," Rachel pleaded. "I care about you."

A dim bedside lamp outlined Anthony's tousled hair as he pulled on a shirt in the open doorway. Rachel stepped around the radio equipment and held on to his arm as if he were the lifeboat and she were drowning.

"From what I hear," he answered, "the Arabs around Kolonia have almost given up already. Only a few old men are left."

"But what is so important about Kolonia that *you* have to be there?"

Anthony sighed and took his wife in his arms.

"This is history, Rachel, and if we're not there to see it, then who knows how it will be told? People have to know the truth. Didn't you say that yourself once?"

"I was wrong," Rachel complained. "Can't you just wait and hear what happens? You could—"

"Everything will be fine." Anthony put his finger to her lips. "Tristan will be coming along with me."

"Tristan . . ." Rachel groaned. "That's even worse."

"And we'll be back in just a few hours with the story of a lifetime. I'm not going to be shooting at anyone, and no one's going to be shooting at me. I'm a journalist, remember?"

"I'd feel better if someone else could go with you—someone who isn't Tristan. What does Tristan know about battles? What does Tristan know about *anything* besides wires and radios?"

Dov had to agree. She had a point there.

"Now you're just worrying," cooed Anthony. "Didn't Yeshua say never to worry?"

"He also said that he who lives by the sword, dies by the sword."

Anthony chuckled. "Touché. I'll leave mine at home. And I wish I could discuss this more with you, Pastor Parkinson, but I must go."

"It's not funny in the least. And I still wish someone else were going with you. Anyone else. You never know what kind of crazy people you'll run into."

Her words sparked a thought. Hadn't Anthony said the Irgun forces might be there? And if Natan was in the Irgun, well . . . After all, there was not much chance of finding his brother if he stayed behind Rachel and Anthony's locked doors. And yet . . .

Anthony would never let me.

"Father," Anthony breathed more quietly, a prayer. "I pray in the name of Yeshua, our Messiah, that you would watch over Rachel while Tristan and I are gone, that you would comfort her heart and let her know you are right beside her. And us, as well. And . . . I pray also for our guest, Dov, that you would show yourself to him, that he would come to know you."

He's praying for me? wondered Dov. *He's about to join a battle, and he's praying for me?*

Dov squeezed his eyes shut and remained death-still as Anthony finished his prayer. It wasn't the first time someone had prayed for him, but he still wasn't used to it. Mr. Bin-Jazzi had prayed that way. He'd talked about the same Messiah, only in his heavy Arabic accent.

The front room was silent for a moment before Anthony walked to the front door. Dov felt a rush of cool night air on his face. But he didn't dare move, could hardly breathe.

"We'll be back before lunch tomorrow," Anthony called back to Rachel softly, but she must have already turned back to the bedroom. Dov heard her quiet sob before two doors clicked shut.

And then the crazy thought returned. No, Anthony would not let him come along. Why would he? Even so . . . Dov jumped from his bed and pulled on his pants almost before he hit the floor. A second later he was out the front door, looking to see which way Anthony had gone.

"Anthony?" Dov whispered into the night. He shivered at the feel of damp stones under his bare feet. Of course, he didn't expect an answer. But a car motor trying to start in the distance told Dov which way to run. He sprinted up three sets of long stone stairways, his shirt and shoes tucked under one arm.

"Anthony!" When Dov was far enough away from Malki Street, he didn't mind shouting out the name. "Wait for me."

He needn't have worried. When he reached the top of the hill, Anthony was still sitting in his car. He didn't notice Dov at first as he slapped the big steering wheel of his Ford and turned the key once more.

Rrr-rrr. The starter growled lower and slower as it sucked the car's battery dry. Anthony nearly jumped through the roof when Dov rapped on the driver's-side window with his knuckles.

"What in heaven's name are *you* doing here?" Anthony rolled down the window.

"I want to go with you." Dov shivered. "Please."

Anthony looked back in the direction of their home. "Does Rachel know you came after me?"

Dov shook his head as he slipped on his shoes. "But she did say you needed someone else to look after you."

"And that would be you?" Anthony chuckled. He turned the key again, but this time the engine only clicked. He hit the steering wheel. "Great. Just great."

Dov knew what to do. He circled around to the back of the car and leaned his shoulder into the wide fender. Anthony let go of the brake and pushed from just behind the open driver's-side door.

"Good!" Anthony yelled back. The tires crunched gravel as they picked up speed. "Just a little faster!"

A moment later Anthony popped the car into gear and the big gray car lurched, then coughed, then roared to life.

"Wonderful, thanks!" Anthony hopped into the moving car and slammed the door behind him. But Dov knew the man wouldn't be able to see him perched down low on the oversized rear bumper, even if Anthony searched his rearview mirror. Dov held on to the rear trunk handle with all his strength, doing his best not to launch to the pavement as Anthony picked up speed through the darkness.

"You've a lot of nerve, young fellow." Anthony stood with his hands on his hips, staring at Dov. He and Tristan had cornered him against the back of the Ford.

"Yeah, sort of like his old uncle Anthony." Tristan grinned over at the other man.

"I am *not* his uncle." Anthony bristled at the teasing. "And he is *not* coming with us. Did you hear that, Dov? There is no way in the world you can be allowed to come along. Don't you know how dangerous this is?"

"That's not what you told Rachel. You said—"

"I know what I said." Anthony wagged his finger. "Don't get impertinent with me."

Dov shrunk back from the scolding, and the look in his eyes must have softened Anthony a bit.

Tristan looked at his wristwatch and ran his fingers through the wild mop of his red, uncombed hair. "Look, Anthony, if we don't get going right now, they're going to leave without us. We're late. So what are you going to do with him?"

"Please don't leave me here." Dov was not above begging, not when tonight was the night he might meet his brother. "I heard Rachel tell you she wished someone else would go with you. Well, that someone is me."

"Say," said Tristan. "Don't I count?"

"You count, Tristan." Anthony paused for a moment, then crossed his arms and spun a half circle away from Dov and Tristan before he yanked open the car door. "I have a feeling I am going to regret this. Get in the car, both of you."

Dov leaped for the open door, but Anthony caught him by the shoulder with two strong hands.

"But you listen to me, Dov. You are going to do everything I say, understand? Everything. If I say drop, you hit the dirt. If you need to stay somewhere, that is precisely what is going to happen. No more games, do you understand?"

Dove saluted. "Yes, sir." This time, he meant it.

BATTLE FOR KOLONIA

"Here." Tristan pointed from his spot in the front seat. "Up here to the right."

That would be the meeting place, as Anthony explained. An armored carload of men sat waiting in an alley on the edge of the quiet Jerusalem suburb. Anthony flashed his lights, and the other car roared away ahead of them in a cloud of smoke.

"That's them." Tristan sounded more like they were going on a school excursion or a hunting trip than to a battle. He kept his window rolled down, despite the air. No one seemed to mind.

And Dov breathed deeply as they sped down the gravel road toward Tel Aviv. It smelled damp and quiet, and the night felt more peaceful than he thought it could possibly be. Nothing at all like a soon-to-be battlefield, but then, maybe it was all a mistake. Frogs croaked in the *wadis*, the valleys that dropped off from the side of the road. A dog barked somewhere off in the shadows as they sped along with their headlights off. Only the flash of a brake light every once in a while from the car ahead guided them along the winding road.

"Does anyone know we're coming?" Dov wondered aloud as they passed dark, sleeping Arab villages. Brooding hills outlined a few low buildings in the faint moonlight.

"I hear the villagers in Kolonia have all left," said Tristan. "The only ones left are the bandits who've been attacking convoys on the highway."

And that's who they would be after. *They*, the Jewish soldiers of the Haganah. Not *they*, two Haganah radio journalists and a boy, all without guns.

Anthony just nodded grimly and kept his attention on the road ahead. Dov held on to the back of the seat, trying not to miss anything. He could feel his heart thumping through his chest.

"Our base is up here," Tristan continued. "By Kiryat Anavim, near that cluster of olive trees. See it?"

Anthony pulled up behind the armored car and parked next to a sheltered field. What had looked like tree stumps turned into soldiers, waiting quietly for their orders.

Dov hopped out with the others. "Is this it?" He looked around for signs of battle. The soldiers hardly noticed the newcomers. Some chatted quietly with each other, and the sound of nervous laughter drifted from several groups. Others oiled their weapons. A few young women circled the meadow, passing out sandwiches and steaming cups of tea.

Anthony rested his hand on Dov's shoulder. "Stay with me. Don't say a word unless I tell you."

"We almost left without you, Parkinson." A squat man with a drab green uniform hopped out of the car ahead and stepped up to meet them. He jerked his head toward Dov. "No one said anything about—"

"He's with me, Yigal," Anthony interrupted. "This is Dov

Zalinski. Works in the station. I will take full responsibility for him."

"Zalinski. I know the name." The soldier's expression did not change much; he spit to the side and motioned to another soldier.

"You do?" Dov perked up. This was why he had come. Someone knew his family name, and maybe his brother, as well!

"Give them helmets," grunted the man, and then paused. "*Three* helmets."

"Wait a minute," Dov panted as the officer turned away. "Do you know my brother?"

But the officer was too busy to answer. He had already barked out instructions to several others. Dov sighed and tried to lean the helmet back enough that he could see out from under the rim.

"Don't ask Yigal any questions," Anthony warned Dov. "He's the commander."

"How's the helmet?" Tristan winked at him. He didn't look much better himself.

"Suits me fine." Dov kept his eyes on the powerful-looking officer. "Just fine."

Twenty minutes later they were ready to march. Actually, *march* was not quite the right word. Rather, two columns of men crept through the night, more like cats than soldiers. The laughing and chatting was left behind in the meadow as they headed toward their goal. One column took the low route, through the twisting wadis. The other followed a few steps behind but higher, up on the ridges. Dov, Anthony, and Tristan were assigned to the rear of the ridge column of silent men.

Actually, *men* was not quite the right word, either. Many, perhaps most of them, weren't more than two or three years older than Dov himself. Each one carried his own stockpile of weapons, though, from rifles and machine guns to grenades. In single file, they crept silently ahead through the barren hills, swirling clouds of ground fog as they advanced. Between the pewter dark and the fog, it looked almost as if they were floating.

"You're supposed to be eighteen to join the Haganah," whispered Anthony, as if he had been reading Dov's mind. "But I think a few of these lads forgot their birth dates. Convenient, eh?"

"I thought they looked a little young." Dov pulled up even with Anthony.

"I wouldn't tell *them* that." Anthony raised his gaze to the mounting hills ahead. Most were barren, except for small groves of olive trees here and there. Dov wondered who tended these trees.

"Jerusalem is up there." Tristan pointed up and straight ahead, where the hills collected in the heights. Less than a half hour by car from Kiryat Anavim, but now a world away. " 'Come, let us go up to Zion,' eh, Dov?"

"Right." Dov had heard the verse before, on the way to Palestine. But he'd never known how truly "up" Jerusalem really was.

"Can you imagine Joshua's men climbing here?" whispered Anthony. "Or Gideon's army, or the Maccabees?"

Stories from the Scriptures, of course. Dov wasn't sure he knew them all, but he shuddered at the sight of a skull-rock, pale and deathly-looking in the scattered moonlight that made it through the clouds. A single shot echoed through the hills, over and over, and he could not tell how close it was, or who had fired it. He shivered at the sound.

"Almost there," whispered Anthony. They'd been walking

for close to an hour behind the long line of men when everyone stopped.

Dov wiped a bead of sweat from his forehead.

Kolonia. No one needed to make the announcement. Behind the soldiers, Dov could just make out a few lonely stone houses, outlined ebony black against the ridgetops. At the wave of an officer's hand, the lower column scrambled to the left, as if they had practiced this. Each soldier seemed to know exactly where to go as they silently circled around to approach from another angle. Dov's group held their position, gripping their weapons tightly. No one said a word. During a pause for breath, Anthony scribbled a few words on a note pad he had produced from his back pocket. Notes for the broadcast?

Dov etched every detail in his mind, too, as if he had his own tablet there. The surefooted movement of their soldiers, like mountain goats on their way to water. The silent hand signals of the officers. The clicking of hundreds of guns, being made ready . . .

And all at once the fireworks began.

Jewish mortars led the attack, filling the air with their screams and booms. Gun or cannon, Dov wasn't sure. He held his ears and watched, spellbound, as the early-morning sky was filled with man-made lightning bolts and the clatter of machine guns.

"Get down!" Anthony forced Dov to the ground with a strong hand to his back. All they could do was watch, listen, count. The soldiers in both columns moved ahead in a crouch, cautiously at first, then more and more confidently. Answering fire came from the village, seeming to fly everywhere but at the Jewish soldiers. In a moment they were running under a blitzing cover of bullets, running toward Kolonia, as if they had planned it that way.

"Amazing," muttered Anthony. He kept scribbling on his pad. At least by the light of the rockets, he would have no trouble seeing what he wrote.

Tristan, on the other hand, had flattened himself into a pancake and was clinging to a rock. He shook and moaned quietly as the shrieks of the mortars thumped against their chests.

"Tristan." Dov shook the young man's shoulder. "Tristan, are you all right?"

Tristan didn't answer, just buried his face in the rock. Big Tristan, the man who had scared Dov so much when they'd first met.

"Listen, Tristan, you don't want them to see you like this." Dov looked around for the soldiers. Most of them had charged the village. It seemed safe enough now, so he tried peeling Tristan from his hiding place. "It's all right."

Tristan swiveled around, his eyes as large as overripe grapefruits. He rose to his feet but stayed hunched over, dusting his pants off. He jumped when another round filled the air with explosions once again.

"Odd." Anthony took a couple of steps toward the action and stopped. He held up his hand as if waiting for a spring rain. "Do you see what's happening?"

"Yeah, we're all going to die is what's happening." Tristan had recovered enough to speak.

But Anthony shook his head. "No, we're not."

"You could have fooled me." Tristan still didn't stand up straight. He shielded his eyes from the blasts.

But Anthony was right. Shots spit out the open windows of one house, then fell silent after another explosion lifted its roof. A hand grenade, Dov guessed. It was the same story for several other small buildings where ragged resistance held out.

But most of the shooting, most of the noise, was over in

half an hour. That's when a soldier came running in their direction, holding a squawking chicken by the legs.

"What's happening?" asked Dov, holding out his hand. It was the first time he'd dared speak above a whisper in the past hour. "Where are all the Arabs?"

The soldier shrugged his shoulders and kept moving. "They ran," he panted. "A lot of the houses were empty. And here's breakfast!"

The soldier proudly held up his catch. Chicken for breakfast? In the distance, one of the stone buildings exploded and tumbled into a heap of dust. Then another, and another. Within sight of Jerusalem, Kolonia was being wiped off the map. The sound of it rolled through the ancient hills and wadis.

"What a waste," mumbled Anthony as they watched the demolition. "I'll bet it's the Irgun boys with their explosives."

Tristan's face looked even more pale than it had before, and Dov shuddered at each explosion. Finally he worked up the courage to ask why the battle had ended this way.

"The bandits will keep coming back if we don't destroy the buildings." Anthony shrugged, but the dark expression in his eyes revealed he was not happy about it, either. He pointed at the ravine below. "For now, we have to keep the highway down there open. And that means keeping attackers and bandits away from Kolonia."

Or what was now left of Kolonia. The rubble had once been homes where people had lived. Homes with families and children. Now even the dogs had run away from the ruins.

And though he looked, Dov did not again see the commander who knew of Natan.

A NEW ANNOUNCER

12

Rachel pulled the boiling water from their kerosene stove and poured another steaming cup of tea for her husband.

"Of *course* you came home with a cold!" she fussed. "Staying out all night, playing army, and what did you expect?"

"Rachel—" Anthony tried to stand up, but she leaned on his shoulder and set the steaming cup in front of him—"the way you talk about it."

"How *else* should I talk about it? And I still can't believe you actually took Dov along. How could you?"

"This thing makes me itch." Anthony clawed at the woolen scarf she had tied around his neck. Evidently, keeping his neck warm was supposed to ward off a sore throat.

"Keep it on," she ordered as Anthony flew into another fit of coughing.

Dov tried to slip his plate quietly onto the kitchen counter, then tiptoed toward the door.

Rachel caught him with her look and a pointed finger. "Wait a minute, you." She wasn't taking no for an answer tonight. Dove held up his hands in surrender. She held a hand to his forehead. "It's a wonder you haven't come down with the same thing, running around in the night air."

"I don't get sick," Dov answered.

"Not this time, perhaps." Rachel looked back to her husband, and Dov had to cover his mouth to hide a grin. Between the hot-water bottle, the tea, and the plaid wool scarf . . .

"What are you laughing at, buster?" Anthony was in no mood for laughs, but Dov was caught, and then he couldn't stop.

"N-n . . ." Dov chuckled, then caught his breath. "Nothing. You just look . . ."

By that time Rachel had caught the giggle, too, as she looked at the way she had dressed her husband. So they laughed and laughed, then laughed and coughed, until tears streamed down Rachel's cheeks.

"Oh dear," gasped Rachel. "I hadn't realized how silly you looked, Anthony."

Anthony gave up trying to sound serious.

"And whose doing is that?" He took a quick sip of his weak English tea. "I am not to blame, my dear."

"Oh, but you're so much fun to dress. Just like a sweet doll I had when I was a girl."

That sent her and Dov into new waves of giggles, until Anthony finally had to give up and laugh along. Dov had no idea he could laugh so; he didn't remember ever trying it before. Had he? He wiped a tear from his cheek with the sleeve of his shirt as a high-pitched squeak sounded from one of the radios in the spare bedroom.

"Oh, my goodness!" Anthony swallowed his grin and looked at the kitchen wall clock. "With all this foolishness, I'd completely forgotten!"

Dov knew right away what Anthony was talking about. Less

than ten minutes to nine. And the nightly broadcast would start at nine o'clock!

"All right." Anthony took another swallow of tea, which only made him cough even more. "I'll . . . be able to . . . read the nightly report."

But Rachel shook her head and picked up the script from the table.

"Listen to yourself, Anthony. You can't."

"No? Then you read it, dear. The broadcast could use a good female announcer."

She dropped the papers as if they burned her fingers.

"Not *this* female. Not me. Absolutely not."

"I take it that's a maybe?"

Avi popped his head in through the kitchen door.

"Five minutes, Anthony."

Anthony got up from the chair. He left his scarf and hot-water bottle on the table.

"We'll be . . ." He cleared his throat. "We'll be right there."

But Rachel wasn't giving up. She stood with her arms crossed, blocking the kitchen doorway.

"I don't know what you're trying to prove, dear. It's too dangerous. Surely your brother or someone else is going to recognize your voice one of these days."

"Surely not the way it sounds now," he croaked, and he had a point. Anthony sounded nothing like his old self. "Besides, the regular announcer will be well enough to come back soon."

"Ooo." Rachel shook her head with disgust.

Dov left them to follow the radio technician into the bedroom studio. At least Tristan had gone home; it wouldn't be as crowded. Avi fiddled with a few knobs on his large black transmitter. A moment later Anthony came breezing in as if nothing had happened.

"All right, Anthony, you'll do fine." Avi hit the standby switch, powered up the transmitter, and looked at his watch. A couple of sausage-shaped glass tubes at the back of the set began to glow a dull yellow gold. Avi adjusted his headset and flicked another row of switches on.

Then they were ready, and Avi opened the nightly broadcast by whistling into the mike. Like everyone else in the country, Dov recognized the eight-bar signature tune from the *"Hatik-vah"*—the Jewish national anthem for a country not yet born.

Anthony took a deep breath, arranged his battle notebook and script . . . and started coughing.

"Are you all right?" hissed Avi, cupping his hand over the microphone.

Anthony gasped and nodded. "This is *Kol Hamegen Haivri*," began Anthony, "the broadcasting service of the Ha-ganah, calling . . ." He turned away from the microphone again to clear his throat once more. ". . . calling on a wavelength of thirty-five to thirty-eight meters, or seven to seven-point-five megacycles. Here is our English transmission."

Avi smiled and gave them the thumbs-up sign, and every-one else relaxed. Rachel unknotted the dish towel she had braided around her knuckles and slid back toward the kitchen with a smile.

"Tonight, a special report from the field," gasped Anthony. His eyes bulged as he stifled another cough. "An eyewitness ac-count of the taking of Kolonia, overlooking the Jerusalem-Tel Aviv highway. Last night . . ."

And that was as far as he got before he erupted in another coughing attack. Rachel returned with a glass of water, but still he could not continue.

"Pardon me," he gasped and pointed at Dov, then at the microphone.

No. Anthony couldn't be serious.

"I and two other companions were able to see the Haganah action firsthand. . . . Here is one of those witnesses, to tell you in his own words . . ."

As another coughing attack seized him, Anthony slid the big metal microphone across the card table to rest in front of Dov. Avi looked as if he was going to faint, but the green light on the front of the radio transmitter stayed on.

"I, ah . . ." Dov wished his tongue would come unglued from his cheeks. "That is, we were part of the force to take Kolonia. I mean, we watched. From the back. Uh, two columns of men set out in the middle of the night . . ."

Anthony nodded and stirred the air with his hand. He said "Go on, Dov" with his nod while he covered another cough.

"The commander was a powerful man, with big arms and a look—well, everyone knew he was in charge." Dov closed his eyes, ignored his shaking hands, and remembered what it had been like, back on the march to Kolonia. "We started out from Kiryat Anavim . . ."

WOOF! Most people jumped when Julian let loose with one of his eardrum-shattering hellos. Emily just patted her dog.

"Do you see him, boy?" she whispered and swallowed. Maybe if she kept a smile on her face, it wouldn't hurt so much.

Or maybe not.

Julian must have noticed Dov before she had, she decided. And she let the big horse of a dog drag her down the sidewalk, away from their home. Even if he was over seventy in dog years, old Julian could still drag her just fine, thank you.

Perhaps Dov was waiting by the bush where he had hidden

before. Yes, that was probably it. Julian gasped and choked as he pulled way ahead. Emily did her best not to trip, or she knew he might drag her down the street face first.

"Slow down, Julian." She gave his collar a jerk. He hardly felt it—not enough to slow down. And then she saw Dov, sure enough, stepping out from behind a Bougainvillaea bush. Julian's tail started spinning.

"I wasn't sure you were going to come." She studied a crack in the pavement.

"It's Thursday night. I said I would, didn't I?"

"I'm afraid you did." Emily bit her lip and handed him a canvas sack. "His bowl, and a couple of bones. Are you sure you're going to be able to feed him? He has a healthy appetite, eats quite a lot. Just about anything, actually. Meat, of course. And apples. He adores apples. Only not too many, or he'll get a stomachache. But no chocolate. Never chocolate."

"What's chocolate?"

She wasn't sure if Dov was serious.

"Never mind. And give him a walk at least once a day. He needs his exercise even though he's old. You promise?"

"Sure, I promise. Say, do you ever listen to the radio?"

"What?"

"No, I suppose you wouldn't."

Emily looked at him sideways before she gave up trying to figure out what he was talking about.

"I wrote down everything you need to know," she told him. "It's in the sack, as well."

"Sure."

"You can read, can't you?"

"What do you mean? Of course I can read. I'm even learning to read English. Your aunt Rachel is teaching me."

Julian sniffed the bottom of the sack, where he must have located the bones.

"He does a few tricks. He shakes, both paws. Show him, Julian. He sits, and stays, when you want him to. You can even balance a dog biscuit on his nose. He's really quite intelligent. You know, my family has had him since he was a puppy, but my father says Great Danes don't live to be much older than ten, so he said it was a good idea for me to leave him here, and—"

"I've never seen a dog biscuit. What do they taste like?"

". . . and I'm afraid he doesn't see too well out of his right eye anymore, but he's still quite good at smelling things. And . . ."

By this time Emily didn't know what she was saying. She couldn't see, either; everything was blurry. She knelt down on the sidewalk, draped her arms around the big dog's neck, and buried her tears in his short fur. She heard the tail go *thunk* on the pavement. And she finally gave up trying to explain everything Dov needed to know.

"You'll be a good dog for me, won't you, Julian?" she whispered, and Julian managed to land a wet dog kiss on her ear. "I'm so sorry we have to leave you here. Will you forgive me?"

Again the tail thunked. Julian would forgive her of anything, she was sure. Everything except what she was about to do.

"I have the leash," Dov told her. "I'll take good care of him for you. Your aunt says the cat won't mind."

"The cat!" Emily straightened up. "Oh dear. I'm afraid I'd quite forgotten about their little black cat."

"She said—"

"Yes, well. I'm sure it will be all right." Emily gave her dog one last squeeze before turning away and standing up. Julian shook himself, as if wondering what all the attention was about, and perhaps when the next biscuit treat was due.

"You *will* take him for walks."

"Sure."

"Promise?"

Dov sighed. "I promise. Don't worry. I'll take good care of him, all right?"

Emily tried to remember if there was anything she had overlooked. Julian panted.

"I do hope you find your brother," she breathed. "I will . . . pray."

WOOF. Julian was ready to play.

"And I promise I'll . . ." She was afraid to say it. "If there's ever any way to find your family—your brother, I mean, or perhaps even your mother, to know what happened to her—I'll do what I can to help, I promise."

"You've already helped. You don't need to do anything else."

"But you're helping me. It's the least I can do."

"Sure." He nodded. He had to know as well as Emily how empty that pledge sounded, but still she felt she had to make it.

Emily ran as fast as she could back down the street, up the stairs, and through the front door. She did not stop; she could not stop.

"Emily?" Her mother wondered as Emily brushed past her in the entry. "Are you going to help me with this box?"

But Emily was already up the stairs and into her empty room. She watched through the curtain as Dov and her dog— *his* dog—disappeared down the street and around the corner.

"Good-bye, Julian," she whispered.

HAIFA ASTERN

13

"Now, look here, old boy. There must be some mistake."

Emily could not remember seeing her father so angry. She scooted over, trying to place herself between Major Parkinson and the unfortunate shipping agent behind the window of the Norsk Lines terminal. Perhaps that way, her father would not strangle the blue-eyed Norwegian man with silvery blond hair and a serious tilt to his face.

"No, sir, I'm sorry. I find no mistake." The Norwegian clerk washed his hands in the air before pointing at his passenger docket. "I have tickets for Miss Emily Parkinson and Miss Constance Pettibone. Cabin 18. I'm afraid there is no ticket for Violet Parkinson. You see? Even if there were, this is a cabin for two, not a cabin for three. My regulations state—"

"Right, you've made that abundantly clear." Major Parkinson's cheeks could have passed for two very ripe tomatoes. "What *I'm* saying is that you must find a place for my wife. She must go with our child on this trip. She simply *must.*"

"This, ah . . . Miss Pettibone will accompany your daughter?"

"Yes, of course, but . . ." He glanced over at Emily's tutor, now drafted to serve as emergency governess. Actually, Constance Pettibone was the latest in a long line of tutors, after Mrs. DeBoer, a Dutch woman; Victoria Wolfe, who had run home to London at the first sign of trouble in Palestine; and the wicked Miss Waterman, whom Emily secretly suspected of having escaped from a women's prison.

The petite Miss Pettibone had obviously never been to prison, nor much out of her fine London neighborhood before coming to Palestine. She still had her pale, almost sickly ivory skin tone, a badge of English superiority worn proudly. And in the short weeks she had served as Emily's tutor, Emily had already given her a private nickname.

Bambi.

One look at the young woman's wide-eyed, amazed stare explained the name. When hunters arrived with a bright torch in the night, Emily was certain Miss Pettibone would stare at the light as she stared now at everything going on around them.

She stared at everyone, from the porters to the men dragging carts piled high with crates to the soldiers coming and going. And Bambi—that is, Miss Pettibone—now stared at the clerk and Major Parkinson.

"I assure you," she cleared her throat. "I am of age."

"Yes, of course, Miss Pettibone," said the major. "I don't believe anyone is questioning your age at the moment."

Emily's mother put her hand on her husband's arm to calm him.

"Alan, you remember we gave our word to this young lady's parents that we would return her with this boat. You remember—"

"I remember it plainly." Major Parkinson chewed on the words before spitting them out. "I'm simply reminding this *fine* fellow that we made reservations for three, and we jolly well are going to load three passengers onto this boat."

"I'm terribly sorry, sir." The Norwegian mopped his forehead with a white handkerchief and replaced it in his vest pocket. "But only Miss Parkinson and Miss Pettibone are allowed to board. There can be no changes. Security regulations, I'm afraid."

"But can't you at least have the girl's mother accompany her instead of her tutor?"

"As I said, no ticket exchanges allowed, I'm afraid."

The major leaned forward, and Emily expected steam to erupt from his ears at any moment.

"No, Alan." Mrs. Parkinson stepped in. "We promised Miss Pettibone's mother, and we're going to keep our word. I can follow them. Perhaps I can get a seat on an airplane. I'll probably even arrive home before them."

"That's not the *point*, Violet. The point is, we were sold three tickets, and now we have a right—"

"As I said, sir." The ticket agent swallowed hard. "There's absolutely nothing I can do. Our regulations state clearly that I am not allowed to make a change."

"But don't you *see*?" The major's ears had turned beet red. Emily took hold of her father's sleeve to try to calm him. "We're only asking you to make it right."

At that, the clerk shrugged and pushed across the two boarding tickets to the *MV Helgefjord*, home port Oslo.

Two boarding tickets, not three.

A loudspeaker announced passengers must board for the 5:15 departure from Haifa Harbor.

Emily looked up at the gleaming white wall clock above the counter. Quarter to five.

"Take the tickets, mister," someone called from behind them in line.

"Alan, we really must get them on the ship," pleaded Mrs. Parkinson, "or *no one's* going to be leaving." She held on to his right arm, Emily to his left. "Please. We have to think about Emily. I want to see her safe in England."

Emily's father freed himself, slapped the counter with his palm, and looked up at the ceiling. Finally he turned back to glare at the hapless clerk.

"Listen, isn't there something I can say to change your mind, eh—what's your name?"

"Haakonsen," replied the tight-lipped clerk. But by this time he had steeled his shoulders and recovered his Scandinavian poise. "Oluf Haakonsen. And I might remind you that the gangplank will be raised in less than fifteen minutes."

"That's very well, Mr. Haak—"

"As I said—" Oluf Haakonsen fixed his iceberg blue Norwegian gaze across the tiny counter—"you can appreciate how our ships are filled to capacity just now."

"Yes, but—"

"And though I dearly wish to help you in this matter, I simply cannot. Would you like me to place your wife on a waiting list for the next sailing?"

"When is that?"

"Three weeks from tomorrow."

"Dear." Mrs. Parkinson leaned over and whispered something in the major's ear. He frowned as he looked from Emily to Miss Pettibone. Emily's mother tugged on his sleeve before he finally sighed, dipped his shoulders in surrender, and nodded.

"We'll be boarding the young ladies, then."

Oluf Haakonsen closed his eyes in relief. And Emily sighed

quietly, unsure how she felt. If she thought about it too much, she would probably start crying. Now she would be traveling back to England with only Miss Pettibone, and not Mum.

"I'm sorry, princess," whispered her father. He turned, picked up two bulging brown suitcases, and walked them toward a loading area.

"It's all right. We'll be fine, Miss Pettibone and I." Emily smoothed a wrinkle in her dark blue traveling dress. She wasn't used to her white hat, however, and its baby's-breath netting made her ears itch.

What a silly thing. She tipped the hat back but kept it perched on her head. Her mother had insisted she wear it, so she kept it on.

"Of course you'll be all right." But Mrs. Parkinson's tears told everyone she wasn't sure. "That isn't the point. The point is, we should have sent you home a long time ago." And then to Emily's tutor: "Now, Miss Pettibone, you will be certain to cable us the moment you arrive in Dover, won't you?"

"Dover?" Miss Pettibone looked at Mrs. Parkinson with wide eyes, as if she'd heard the plan for the first time. A crane lowered last-minute supplies from the Haifa pier, while men shouted back and forth in three languages. A crate crashed on deck, to the great excitement of a number of workers.

"Miss Pettibone?" Emily's father tried to get the tutor's attention.

"Oh yes, sir, of course." Miss Pettibone snapped back to attention. "I'll certainly write you from London."

"No, no. Cable from Dover. Do you understand?"

Emily gave her father a look from behind Miss Pettibone's back, to let him know she understood just fine. Miss Pettibone nodded feebly.

"All right." He nodded. "You're off, then. Shouldn't be more than a few days, and you'll be home."

Home. Emily hugged her parents before climbing the long ramp to enter the ship. If home was where Mum, Daddy, and Julian were, then she wasn't going home at all.

She was leaving it.

"Now, remember," her father called out to them as they climbed, "be sure to write—"

The rest of his words were cut off by the long, low blast of a steam whistle.

"I will!" Emily tried to look back over her shoulder, but the thick-armed Arab porters carrying her bags now blocked the way. Miss Pettibone looked dizzy, her knuckles white on the side railing.

"Your tickets, please?" The uniformed man at the top of the gangway sounded like Oluf Haakonsen's twin brother. Emily lifted her shoes to keep from tripping and handed up her papers. She did not look back again until a quarter hour later, when she leaned over the upper-deck railing of the *Helgefjord* and tried to pick out her parents in the crowd on the Haifa pier.

"Do you see them?" Emily saw a hat that looked like her mother's. She held on to her own in the freshening breeze.

Bambi shook her head no.

"Oh, there!" Emily waved wildly when she saw her parents, who were shading their eyes against the setting sun and waving just as wildly. "There they are!"

She blew them a kiss and tried in vain not to cry. As the men loosened the big ship's mooring lines, the *Helgefjord* gave a little shudder. The thundering steam whistle blew again, and a stiff Mediterranean breeze made Emily pull her knit wrap over her shoulders.

I am never going to see my home again.

"If I never see this horrid desert again," announced Miss Pettibone, dabbing her nose with a lace-fringed handkerchief, "it will be too soon."

Emily didn't reply. How could someone like Bambi ever understand?

"I am going inside," sniffed Emily's tutor. "It's entirely too chilly out here."

Or too sunny, or windy, or . . .

"You go ahead." Emily nodded and shivered. "I'll be right along. Perhaps we can explore the ship together."

But Emily wasn't right along. She stood glued to the railing as a trio of grimy tugs pushed their ship out into Haifa Harbor. On the pier, the send-off crowd dwindled as black coal smoke billowed out the *Helgefjord*'s tall red-and-blue smokestack. Emily stood where she was until the last few people on the pier looked like ants, still waving.

"Good-bye, Mum, Daddy," she whispered to the wind. "Good-bye, Julian." A gull had followed them out to sea, barely flapping its gray wings as it banked in the wind.

"And good-bye, Dov."

She waved back as Palestine's low shore began to fade and swells caught the ship in a gentle, rocking lullaby. At the same time, a fresh wind caught her hat and sent it sailing out over the waves.

"Oh!" she cried, surprised but not quite disappointed. In fact, it seemed just the right touch. Her sea-gull friend inspected the hat, perhaps thinking it a meal, but turned away when he found he couldn't eat the netting. Emily finally turned away, as well, but she was nearly bowled over as Miss Pettibone rushed out to the deck. Bambi's face looked properly green.

"Are you quite all right?" asked Emily.

Miss Pettibone waved her away, so Emily stepped into the

warmth of the main passenger lounge. A few of the other passengers were sitting on comfortable chairs, chatting and listening to a wireless. No one else looked as seasick as Miss Pettibone, and no one seemed to notice as the radio announcer whistled the first few notes from the "Hatikvah." But something about the radio announcer's voice made Emily stop in her tracks.

"This is Kol Hamegen Haivri, the broadcasting service of the Haganah," said the announcer, "calling on a wavelength of thirty-five to thirty-eight meters, or seven to seven-point-five megacycles. Here is our English transmission."

"Does anyone care to hear this rubbish?" A middle-aged man with a smoldering pipe in his hand stood to adjust the set. "I'd wager most of us have had our fill of their troubles. Let the Jews and the Arabs fight it out, I always say. I for one will be right glad to get back to proper British soil."

"Hear, hear." A few other people nodded their agreement. But as he reached for the dial, Emily held up her hand.

"Wait a moment!" She felt her face flush. "I'd like to hear it. Please?"

"Oh." The man turned to stare at Emily, then bowed his head. "Beggin' the young lady's pardon."

NEVER GIVE UP

14

The radio broadcast continued, surprisingly clear, considering they were a few miles offshore by now. Clear enough for Emily and the others to hear every word her uncle Anthony said over the next several minutes.

"I bring you part two in our eyewitness accounts of the fighting at the Arab village of Kolonia," he said. Anthony stifled a cough but went on. "Fighting was fierce but brief, lasting no more than thirty minutes. One Haganah soldier was killed, three wounded, while up to sixteen Arabs were killed. Leaders of the Haganah strike team said that Arab forces quickly abandoned the site and have taken up a new position on the other side of the highway, so food and supply convoys between Tel Aviv and Jerusalem will still have a hard time getting through."

Even the man with the mustache was listening now as Anthony paused. Emily thought she heard whispering in the background, a shuffling of papers, more coughing.

"People all over the country have been wondering what a battle like this might mean," he continued. "Only one thing. It means that Jews and Arabs must find a way to settle their differences, without killing each other. And so we will continue this fight for the truth on these broadcasts so that everyone can hear, and so the fighting can end."

Emily felt a strange warmth inside, listening to her uncle talk about other news in their country. She wanted to shout to all the others, "That's my uncle!" but of course didn't dare. Even so, the others listened until he started to wrap up the short broadcast.

"And here is a personal message to Natan Z from Warsaw. Your brother, Dov, is alive and would like to meet with you at the Montefiore Windmill at sundown. And now, this is the English transmission of Kol Hamegen Haivri, the broadcasting service of the Haganah, signing off."

They're not giving up, thought Emily, with a silent prayer that Natan Z would hear his brother's plea to meet in Jerusalem. Already, Jerusalem felt so very, very far away.

Dov looked up at the armless windmill Sir Moses Montefiore had built in 1857 as a way for Jews to make a living in the Holy Land. A flour mill, Anthony had told him. He pulled up his collar as the Friday-night darkness—and the Sabbath—crept closer.

How silly of me, thought Dov. *Even if Natan hears the broadcast, why would he come?*

Anthony had agreed to repeat the message twice more. After that, well . . . They all knew the chances of Natan hearing it were slim.

No, Natan probably hadn't been listening, or maybe he didn't care to meet his long-lost brother at the foot of the windmill. At least, he hadn't shown up for the past two evenings.

Maybe he just couldn't get away from whatever he was doing, thought Dov. *Maybe.*

Still, Dov stayed at his post by the windmill, on the lookout for his brother, for his past. He shuffled his feet and looked behind him for British soldiers.

In a small upper window, one of their neighbors had lit two candles to mark the beginning of *Shabbat,* the Jewish Sabbath. Even as the fighting grew worse and the bullets flew, these Jews held tightly to their customs, their Sabbath candles, their traditional *challah* bread and prayers. The only difference was, these candles sat perched on top of two sandbags.

But the Arabs in the valley below obviously didn't share the candlelighting mood. This Sabbath's prayers were joined by a new volley of gunfire, more faded shouts of *"Allah Akhbar!"* or "God is great!" Dov wasn't sure what God had to do with any of this shooting and fighting. He covered his head and dove behind a low stone wall.

"Here it comes again!" Dov whispered to himself. The shots would echo through the streets, a baby would cry, the people of Yemin Moshe would go on with their evening prayers. The men would meet down at the neighborhood synagogue, the building that perched almost right on the valley rim, nearly in the line of fire. It was an odd thing to get used to, this everyday living in the midst of battle.

Dov passed the time counting shots and wondered how long it would be before Rachel or Anthony discovered he was still gone and came looking for him.

The shooting continued, several shots ricocheting off a corner of the building above his head.

"Where are you, Natan?" Dov covered his face as another shot plowed into a window above. Sand trickled down the wall, as if the building were bleeding.

"Dov?"

Dov turned to see Anthony, hurrying hunched down toward his hiding place.

"Dov? Are you still out here?"

Dov raised his hand and whistled softly, bringing Anthony in like a warplane looking for a safe landing spot.

"Don't you know it's dangerous?" he huffed. Anthony rolled into place behind the wall. "Rachel and I were worried."

"They haven't shot at the windmill before. I thought it would be safe here."

"Well, it's not anymore." More shots. An Arabic shout echoed in the valley below. "Let's get back home. We'll look for your brother another time."

Maybe Anthony was right. Natan wasn't coming. And Dov would have followed if he hadn't seen the shadow moving on the other side of the windmill. A wiry skeleton of a man crossed the courtyard between them. Strolled, actually, as if he couldn't hear the shots whizzing overhead. They both stared in wonder.

"He's either deaf," whispered Anthony, "or he's absolutely crazy."

This couldn't be Natan . . . could it?

It occurred to Dov that he might not recognize his brother even if he met him face-to-face. Natan would be eighteen or nineteen, Dov supposed—he wasn't quite sure. This stranger looked about that age. He stood in front of them, staring from the other side of the low stone wall.

Dov stared back. This wasn't the way family reunions were supposed to happen; he knew that much. And Dov had the odd feeling of looking straight into a mirror. He saw the same nose and cheekbones as his own, the same dark hair that stood on end, and the same eyes . . . There was no mistake. But did Dov's eyes look that empty, too?

"I never thought I'd see you again, Dov." The gravelly voiced stranger crossed his arms just as another volley of shots shrieked over their heads.

"Get down, man!" ordered Anthony. "You'll be killed!"

STRANGER FOR A BROTHER

15

Never mind the bullets that filled the air on this dangerous corner of the Yemin Moshe neighborhood. Natan only held out his left hand, palm up, as if he was testing for a drop of rain. Satisfied, he dropped his hand and stood his ground. After a few minutes the shooting stopped.

"You're the Haganah radio voice." He looked at Anthony. It was not a question.

"Yes." Anthony coughed a bit, not as bad as before, though his voice was still hoarse. "I'm Anthony Parkinson, but—"

"Nice *British* name," Natan growled.

"Natan?" Dov's voice cracked as he slowly rose to his feet. "You came."

"Yeah, I came." He kept his gaze focused on Anthony, never smiling.

"I didn't think you would. I was hoping, but—"

"I wasn't sure I would, either." Natan shrugged. "But I can't stay long."

A stray bullet hit the windmill, showering them with splin-

123

ters. Anthony and Dov ducked for cover, while Natan stayed still.

"Not very good shots," he chuckled.

Dov wasn't sure if he should hug his long-lost brother or wrestle him to the pavement. How long had he waited for this moment? How many years? And now his brother took crazy risks and couldn't stay long.

"If we were in charge, this wouldn't be happening." Natan was obviously done with hellos. He motioned toward the valley below.

"And who exactly is 'we'?" asked Anthony. Dov hadn't heard that kind of sharp edge to Anthony's voice before.

Natan grinned and ignored the question, but he seemed to enjoy the challenge.

"We'd have the Hinnom Valley secure in a day or two, Brits or no Brits."

"Of course. I assume you'll have Shabbat dinner with us?" Anthony's invitation seemed forced, his voice tinged with a serious case of frostbite. Dov knew that whatever he had expected, this was not a good start.

But Natan just squinted at his watch and then studied them, like a dog-show judge trying to decide a mutt's pedigree. He pulled at his chin, then nodded.

"I have an hour to spare. Why not?"

They followed him around the corner without another word; Natan seemed to know precisely where the Parkinsons lived.

Anthony hung back for a moment to whisper into Dov's ear. "Do you have any idea who your brother really is?" he hissed.

"What do you mean?" Dov gave him a puzzled look.

"He's in the Irgun. A terrorist."

"How can you be sure?"

"Trust me, Dov. Do you see that gun tucked into his belt?"

His brother? A terrorist like the ones who had once kidnapped Emily Parkinson?

Rachel must not have cared, or at least she did not appear to. Maybe she was just used to unexpected dinner guests. After a quick glance at her husband, she beamed and set another plate on their little dining-room table. Her own two candles in the window glowed almost as cheerfully as her smile.

"We've heard so much about you, Natan. Of course, we were praying Dov would find you. Or that you would find Dov."

"Oh." Natan settled his light frame on the edge of a chair and looked around the snug home. The bedroom door was tightly closed. "Does that mean you're . . . observant?"

Observant. That meant the most religious Jews, the ones who *observed*, or kept the Old Testament laws. The ones who lit their Sabbath candles exactly eighteen minutes before sundown.

"We're Messianic Jews." Rachel's smile warmed up the room as she placed a loaf of braided *challah* bread in front of her guest. "Or I mean, *I* am. Anthony is a Messianic Anglican, so to speak."

Natan acted as if he didn't understand.

"We believe the Messiah has already come," she continued. "Yeshua. Jesus. And we'd love to tell you about Him, if you want to know. Will you ask the blessing, Anthony?"

Dov kept an eye on his brother, who in turn kept an eye on him and on the Parkinsons, who bowed their heads and closed their eyes after they had found their chairs.

"Blessed are you, O Lord our God, who provides us bread from the earth," said Anthony in a soft voice. "And we thank you, Lord, for Yeshua, the Bread of Life, through whom we have eternal life."

Natan seemed comfortable enough with the prayer, until Anthony tore off a piece of the loaf and added his own P.S. at the end.

"And, Father, we thank you for bringing together brothers who have not known each other for so long. We pray for the peace of Jerusalem, that all this useless fighting would stop, that your will may be done in the lives of Natan and Dov. In the name of the Messiah Yeshua, amen."

"Eat, eat!" Rachel didn't give anyone a chance to react. Maybe she, like Dov, had seen Natan begin to back away in his chair.

Rachel put a hand on Anthony's shoulder. "I hope that wasn't too much salt," she told her husband in a low voice.

"Salt?" asked Dov. "In the challah bread?"

"Not that kind of salt." Rachel laughed. "Rav Sha'ul once wrote that our speech should always be seasoned with salt. A bit of salt makes you thirsty to hear more, isn't that right, Anthony?"

"Rav Sha'ul means Paul," Anthony translated. "A famous rabbi in the Scriptures."

Dov still wasn't sure who Rav Sha'ul was, but he thought he got the point.

"But it's your turn, Natan." Anthony finally offered a smile. Maybe the meal was softening him up. "Tell us what happened for you to come here. The Lord must have intended for you to hear the broadcast so you'd find us."

"I heard it, all right." Natan took another bite and glanced over at Dov. "I also hear the Brits are still looking for your station."

He looked hungry enough to stay now, especially after Rachel had brought out more food: canned Australian asparagus soup, dried herring from Turkey, strawberry jam, and hot Earl Gray tea. She seemed proud of herself for having found such treasures in a city with less and less to eat. Sammy, Rachel's cat, set up station under the table while Julian whimpered at the back door.

"Julian, hush!" Dov wanted to hear Natan tell them more. But Natan told them little about himself, except that he had worked as a mechanic in a machine shop in Tel Aviv since the war and now was staying for a while in Jerusalem.

"Always one step ahead of the Brits," he chuckled without smiling. "They haven't been able to catch up with me yet—not Natan Israeli."

"That's it." Anthony snapped his fingers and put down his fork. Everyone looked at him. "I've been trying since Dov first mentioned you to figure out why your name seemed oddly familiar. You helped three Irgun terrorists escape Acre Prison last month, didn't you? Natan Israeli. You're a wanted man."

The cat purred, but no one else dared speak.

A small grin played at the corners of Natan's mouth.

So Anthony is right about Natan!

Still Dov listened, trying his best to mask the sinking feeling in the pit of his stomach. If *this* was an answer to prayer, as Anthony and Rachel had said, then it was as unwelcome as a hand-me-down shirt that pinched his shoulders and made his back itch. Wasn't his long-lost brother supposed to greet him with open arms and stories of their parents? If Dov had known Natan was going to be like this . . .

"What about *Imma* and *Abba*, Natan?" He couldn't hold back the question any longer. "Why don't you tell me about our parents?"

Natan looked around the table for a long moment before

he shrugged his shoulders. Finally he took a deep breath. And for the first time, his tough-guy mask showed tiny cracks.

"Not much to tell. Abba was sick during the war. Real sick. We thought he was going to die, but of course, a lot of other people died, too." He took another sip of his soup, as if he had all the time in the world to tell his story. "We had nothing to eat, and what we had, Abba gave it all to us. Even what *he* should have eaten. One day he went out to find some food, and he . . . he never came back. The Nazis must have rounded him up."

No one said a word.

"But he must have survived the war somehow. Like me, I guess. All the way through the war, can you believe it? Don't ask me how."

Natan took a deep breath, and the blaze in his eyes told Dov he was more angry than grieved. "I heard he died on Cyprus in a stinking British detention camp."

Dov nodded slowly. "I heard that, too."

"How?"

"I have a friend who's Br—I mean, who knows. But what about Imma?"

Natan rested his forehead in his hand and took another deep, ragged breath.

"I never found out what happened to her after we were separated. I searched. I asked. All over Warsaw, all over Poland, all over Europe, all over everywhere.

"But nobody I ask knows anything about her. If she's still alive, I'm pretty sure she's not here in Eretz Israel."

"We, ah . . ." Rachel looked at Anthony for help. "Perhaps you boys would rather discuss this kind of thing later by yourselves?"

"Later?" The word seemed to ignite him. Natan threw

down his napkin and stood up. "There is no *later*. The Jews had no *later* in the Warsaw ghetto. No *later* in the Nazi death camps, or the British camp on Cyprus. And now there is no later for us here!"

"I'm sorry, of course I didn't mean—" Rachel tried to apologize, but this houseguest would have none of it.

"Look through your front windows! While you sit here playing with your Haganah radio, families are being attacked behind the Old City walls. Can you hear them?"

"Now, see here," Anthony objected. "It's tough for everyone. You have no right—"

But Rachel rested her hand on his arm to interrupt as Natan went on.

"They're right across the Valley of Hinnom, and here you sit, while Jews are trapped like rats by the British—just so they can be attacked every night by the Arabs. Do you hear them? I do. And your Haganah commander says there's nothing we can do to help them. No way to get in."

"We're doing all we can," insisted Anthony.

"So why are they starving in there? Not enough food. Not enough supplies. Not enough men and ammunition. I tell you, if I could be in there, behind those walls, that's where I'd be. Defending the wall. Defending the city!"

Dov followed the argument like a tennis match across the table, back and forth, and the volleys grew more and more fierce.

"Don't you think I've thought of that, too?" Anthony's cheeks turned red.

"Why would you? You're not Jewish. You're British! I don't know why the Haganah let you in. How would you understand anything?"

"You don't have to like me, but I understand much more than you might think."

"Dear, please." Rachel tried to hold her husband back.

He shrugged her off. "I'm all right." Anthony straightened his sleeves and checked his wristwatch. "I just want him to know that the Haganah and the Irgun want the same thing. We just go about it in different ways. Someday soon we'll all be fighting together."

"Haganah? Fight? The Irgun are the only Jews who know how to fight."

"I don't think so. We have other ways of fighting."

"Like what, for example?"

"Like . . . well, we've thought for weeks about trying to get our portable field transmitter inside the Old City. That back-pack-sized radio." He pointed at a bundle in the corner of the living room, behind the couch. "Can you imagine what we could do if we could just broadcast a few reports from inside? The whole world would know the truth!"

Natan laughed—a dry, sad chuckle. "And then what?" He looked unconvinced.

Anthony leaned back in his chair, pressed his hands to his face, and closed his eyes.

"I can see we're never going to agree on this." Anthony sighed. "Listen, Natan, I'm not saying we won't have to defend ourselves. All I'm saying is, well, there's more to it than that."

The room again turned very quiet. Dov heard himself swallow the bite of herring he had been chewing for the past couple of minutes. Where was the cat when you needed him?

Natan turned to Rachel. "Thank you for the excellent dinner, Mrs. Parkinson. I'm sorry you had to share it with an Irgun terrorist like me." When his voice quieted, Dov could almost remember the sound of it, a faint memory from when he was little, before the war. But so very faint.

Rachel's face paled, and she started to say something, but she must have changed her mind.

Natan went on. "And you, little brother." When he looked straight at Dov, the sadness in his eyes was overpowering. "Maybe memories are better than the real thing sometimes. I'm sorry to disappoint you."

"No." For a moment Dov studied his brother's rough, hardened face, the one so much like his own. He wished he could say something to bring his brother back to the table, to erase the anger of the past ten minutes and the nightmares of the past ten years. Could he say something besides no?

Natan turned to go.

Dov rose to his feet and followed, not ready to say goodbye. "I know how you can get into the Old City." The words were out of Dov's mouth before he knew what he was saying. Natan stopped in his tracks. "What did you say?" He swiveled slowly to face Dov once more.

Why am I telling him this? Dov asked himself.

"I said, I know how you can get into the Old City."

But then it was back to the old Natan, the one he had met by the windmill. "How could you possibly know something like that?"

"I just do, that's all."

"All right, then." Natan crossed his arms in a challenge. "So tell me."

"I can't tell you." Dov shook his head. "But I can show you."

UNDERCOVER
16

At first Emily thought the sun on her face felt good, streaming in through the small round porthole. She stretched on her narrow bunk and tried to smell the salt air, tried to imagine where they might be or if they might have passed the toe of Italy in the night. The distant *thrum-thrum* of the ship's powerful engines sounded from somewhere deep below.

But then she stiffened.

Wait a moment. She looked around the tiny cabin, first at Miss Pettibone, still snoring loudly on the other bunk, with her black mask over her eyes and earplugs in her ears, snuggled up against the outside wall with a silver bucket next to her on the floor, just in case.

But Emily was pretty sure Miss Pettibone's snoring hadn't woken her up. The sun in her eyes was the culprit. Emily propped herself up on one elbow and glanced up at the window once more.

If the sun is coming in our window, she thought, *and we're on the starboard side of the ship—the right side—then we must be sailing . . .*

North?

That can't be right. Emily dressed quietly, ran a brush through her hair, and slipped out the door as she knotted a kerchief in place. *Why would we be sailing north instead of west?*

It didn't take long to find out. Out on deck, a cluster of deckhands leaned over the forward railing. A couple were staring at something just ahead with binoculars.

"Oh my!" Emily gasped at the sight of black smoke rising off the water. She had thought they'd left such things behind, back in Jerusalem.

"What's happening here?" she asked, joining the men at the railing. Just then she felt the waves changing under her feet as the ship slowed.

"Looks like we'll be taking on a few more passengers." A young man with a junior officer's peaked cap pointed down at the waves ahead, in the direction of the smoke cloud. "We had to backtrack a few hours to find them, though."

That's when Emily saw what all the excitement was about: a small fishing cutter, burning probably from the engine room, leaning dangerously to the side. And the people! Refugees, obviously, by the rags they wore. To Emily, it looked like more people than boat—she counted over seventy-five, maybe one hundred, as the *Helgefjord* drew closer.

"We're bringing them aboard!" another young officer called out as he trotted down from the wheelhouse. "British command says they're illegal Jewish immigrants."

Some of the immigrants had already jumped from their sinking ship, but the men at the *Helgefjord's* railing yelled and waved at them not to swim closer.

"Get them aboard!" shouted the officer as some of his crew threw rope ladders over the side.

Emily stood frozen, watching the drama. "Are they coming with us?" she asked.

"Only a short ways," the officer replied. "We're taking them to the British holding camp in Cyprus."

"How do I look?" Natan arched his eyebrows as they hurried through the narrow Old City street.

"Shh. Like a Polish Jew with a fake Arab *kaffiyeh.*"

"Oh, come on." Natan adjusted the white Arab-style headdress. "This is supposed to look like the real thing."

"It does look like the real thing. Just like this crate of oranges. Now be quiet, or you'll give us away."

"You've got a lot of *chutzpah* talking to me the way you do."

"You had a lot of nerve talking to Anthony the way *you* did."

"Yeah, well, speaking of that Gentile, I'm surprised he let you borrow his precious field transmitter. Was that your idea?"

Dov didn't answer. It was.

"Oh, I see. Did you even tell him you were going to meet me here?"

"I left them a note. He wouldn't have let me come."

"*Let* you? You talk about Anthony as if he were your father."

"You know he's not."

"Huh. You're crazier than I thought. They've got you brainwashed."

"Brainwashed? What are you talking about?"

"The whole radio thing. The truth will set you free, and all that. You really believe that?"

"Maybe."

Maybe? Dov adjusted the wooden crate on his shoulder and

tried not to think of how he had tiptoed out of Rachel and Anthony's apartment at dawn—after Natan had eaten Sabbath dinner with them the night before. Meeting Natan just outside the Damascus Gate was the easy part. Now, here in the Muslim Quarter, came the hard part. He hoped the carefully stenciled *CITRUS: PRODUCT OF PALESTINE* in both English and Arabic would keep anyone from discovering the portable radio transmitter inside.

"Where did you ever find that barking elephant you keep in the back garden? He's a monster."

"A friend gave him to me. But Julian is okay. Rachel will take care of him, and I'll be back later today."

"You will, as long as you know the way, kid."

"I'm not a kid. And of course I know the way."

He did. Ha Shal-shelet, the Street of the Chain, was only three short blocks ahead. But Dov stiffened as they approached a patrol strolling their way.

"Friends of Anthony's?" asked Natan. Of course they wouldn't be, though they were British.

"Don't look at them," Dov whispered back. This time he didn't think his older brother would have any trouble following his instructions. And he tried to keep from running as they passed by on the other side of the narrow lane. Maybe the soldiers wouldn't notice.

No such luck.

"Say, hold on, there." The leader of the patrol, a broad-faced sergeant, waved his men over. "Are those oranges you've got there, or hand grenades?"

A couple of the soldiers chuckled. Dov tried to pretend he didn't understand, and hugged the stone wall as he attempted to walk by. How would a young Arab boy act in a situation like this?

The sergeant managed to place a big black boot in his way. "I said, hold up there, lad. Let's have a look."

The soldier motioned with his hand and pointed to the crate. They had no choice but to stop in the middle of the road.

Dov's ears pricked up when his older brother whispered into his ear in Yiddish: "Ditch the stupid radio. Throw the box at the big one, and we run in different directions."

Dov smiled at the soldier and shook his head. At least two soldiers blocked their way in either direction. All had rifles slung low over their shoulders, and the shark-eyed look on their faces told him they might welcome a chance to use them.

"No," Dov whispered back. "I can't."

"Eh, what's that?" The big soldier stomped on the crate with the toe of his boot, grabbed Dov's shoulder, and raised a pistol with his free hand. "No whispering."

"*Salaam!*" Dov gave them his biggest smile and put on his best Arabic-flavored English. "Peace. Oranges. For you."

With that, he reached into his crate and pulled out one of the few pieces of precious fruit they'd used to cover the top of the radio.

If they find this, he thought, *we're in trouble. And Natan is in bigger trouble.*

Dov knew it might already be too late, as one of the other soldiers eyed them closely. He even pointed out Natan to one of the other soldiers, and they whispered among themselves.

"Hmm." The sergeant held the orange to his nose and took a deep whiff. "One for each of us, and then you're on your way."

Dov put himself between his brother and the curious soldiers, making sure he blocked their view as best he could. Then, one at a time, he tossed an orange to each of the other six soldiers.

I don't have enough! He glanced over at Natan. Maybe they would have to run, after all.

"Not for me." The sixth soldier, a young pimple-faced recruit, held up his hand. "Too sour."

Dov nodded and slid the top of the crate into place before hefting the radio back to his shoulder.

"Go on, then," the soldier ordered them.

Gladly. Dov didn't wait for the sergeant to change his mind but hurried away on a narrow lane as fast as he could. As soon as they dared, they turned into the quiet shadows of a blind alley.

"They didn't recognize you," Dov told his brother, catching his breath. "Why not?"

"I haven't the slightest idea." Natan looked back over his shoulder. "But why didn't you do as I said?"

"You mean run? I'm not stupid. They had guns, or maybe you didn't notice."

"Oh, so you're scared of British guns."

"I'm not scared. What is it with you?"

Natan rolled his eyes. "I don't know why I'm listening to you."

"Because I'm the one who knows a way into the Jewish Quarter, and you don't."

"I could find my own way."

"Listen, you!" Dov faced his brother now with a clenched fist, ready to pound some sense into him, if that's what it took. "I didn't like the way you talked to Anthony and Rachel. And I don't like the way you talk to me. You're about as arrogant as they come. Worse than Emily Parkinson."

"Don't you threaten me." Natan pointed his chin at Dov's face. "And who's Emily Parkinson?"

"Never mind. But if you want me to take you through the

tunnel, you're going to have to do exactly what I say."

Natan looked away for a moment, glancing up at an old woman hanging wash out her second-story window. "For now, little brother. Just for now. So show me the way to your Arab scum friend's shop."

Never mind the heavy box on his shoulder. Dov flew at his brother with his free hand and a red-eyed vengeance.

"Don't you ever call him that!"

Dov missed his first swing and lost his balance.

"Relax, will you?" Natan danced backward and caught the crate to keep it from falling, and they twirled in a sort of awkward dance. They ended up nearly face-to-face, the way Natan and Anthony had earlier. But Natan held the considerable weight of the crate while Dov gripped his brother's neck.

"You want to let go of my neck?" Natan wheezed.

Dov simmered, but didn't let go.

"Not until you take back what you said about Mr. Bin-Jazzi."

"Nothing personal, all right? It's just that I generally don't get along with Arabs."

"Sure, not all of them are friendly toward us, but there's nothing wrong with Arabs. And you're in the wrong neighborhood to be saying things like that, I hope you know. Who *do* you get along with?"

"Not you."

"Obviously. You hate everybody, don't you?"

Natan finally flipped Dov aside, sending the younger boy sprawling. He tossed the crate into Dov's lap.

"You've got a lot to learn."

Dov got to his feet slowly. "You know what I wish?"

"I don't care what you wish."

And Dov didn't care that his brother didn't care. He hoisted the radio back onto his shoulder.

"I wish I'd never tried to find you!"

"Well, it looks as if we're stuck with each other for the time being."

Dov was quiet as he led the way out to Ha Shal-shelet.

"Spasiba." A young mother nodded at Emily and pulled a blanket over the shoulders of her little girl. "Thank you."

Emily smiled and poured another cup of hot soup for the next person huddled in the open cargo area. Never mind that Miss Pettibone refused to come near the refugees or that Emily couldn't understand the Russian they spoke. A few English words filtered out here and there, "thank you," and "please," and the like. This was a way Emily could help. A way she could forget she was alone with no one but Miss Pettibone. And it made her feel good to see the smallest of the children smile up at her.

"Do they understand where we're taking them?" Emily whispered to the cook's assistant, who had hurriedly brought them the soup kettle.

He rubbed the dragon tattoo on his forearm, flexed his muscle to make it wiggle, and shrugged. "Dunno, miss."

And you probably don't care, either. Emily didn't dare say it out loud. But she shivered to think of the British holding camp on Cyprus, perhaps not much better than the camps in which a few Jews had survived the war. A baby cried on the other side of the big room, and Emily didn't blame her a bit. She might have joined in if a boy with a runny nose and big blue eyes hadn't put out his hands for his soup.

"There you go." She handed the toddler a bowl and smiled

again, but only on the outside. On the inside . . .

Someone had set up a shortwave radio receiver on a shelf near the door, but most of the refugees had drifted away after the special daytime Hebrew broadcast had ended a few minutes earlier. Now Emily was one of the only ones in the crowded room who could understand English.

"Uncle Anthony." The sound of her uncle's still-hoarse voice brought a strange touch of home to the now-crowded ship.

"An-ton-eee?" repeated the little boy at her feet, studying her face.

"Yes, you see, that's my uncle Anthony on the radio, reading the news." Emily said the words, though she knew he wouldn't understand.

"Noose?" repeated the boy.

"I'm sorry." She tried to listen to her uncle, but the Russian voices around her were too loud. That, and the coughing, the crying of children, a mother singing a soft Russian lullaby. In between all the noise, her uncle Anthony sounded very distant, indeed.

He told about another riot in Ramallah and clashes on the Tel Aviv-Jerusalem highway at Abu Gosh. He told, too, of food shortages in Jerusalem getting worse every day because the truck convoys still couldn't get through. She listened to the words as if they came from another planet, and then to the announcements at the end of the broadcast. Rivkah sent her greetings to her family in Neve Yaacov and to her mother in Atarot. Avigdor wanted very much for his family in Kfar Uriya not to worry; he was well. And there were others.

"And, Dov . . ." Emily's uncle paused for just a moment before he finished his broadcast, "we'd like very much for you to return home."

A bowl of soup slipped from Emily's fingers and clattered to the metal deck.

"Ey!" The toddler danced out of the way, and a few mothers glanced at her with worried eyes.

"Oh dear." She fell to her knees and tried to mop up the mess with a hand towel. The little Russian boy seemed happy to help her. "Dov, where are you now?"

"Sorry, sorry, we're closed!" Mr. Bin-Jazzi jumped up and intercepted the customer who had just stepped into the little shop. "I'll get you your spices tomorrow, Mrs. Rashid."

With that, the powerful little man twirled Mrs. Rashid on her heel and led her back out the door. He slammed it and shoved the bolt across.

"An extra something I've put on the door, since the troubles began." He frowned for a moment, then brightened. "Are you sure you boys won't have some coffee? You're my guests. You must have some coffee."

"I'll get it, *Abu*—" Dov began. *Does Mr. Bin-Jazzi have any coffee?*

"Not this time. I'm just so pleased you're back, and that you found your brother. It's an answer to prayer, is it not? Finally you have found your family. This is a good thing!"

Dov looked at his brother. An answer to prayer? A good thing?

Mr. Farouk Bin-Jazzi scurried up the stairs to the upper room while Natan leaned forward on his elbows at the card table.

"Where do you find all these religious fanatics, Dov? Don't tell me . . . a Messianic Arab?"

"I guess you could say that."

Natan hit his head. "Oy, I was just kidding, okay? If you don't watch out, all this Messianic stuff is going to rub off on you. I'm telling you, Dov."

"So what do you care? Maybe it already has." Dov surprised himself with his own words. Had it really rubbed off? Had the "salt" Rachel and Anthony and others sprinkled into their talk really made him thirsty?

"Look, I don't have time for this, Dov. Show me the tunnel, and let's get out of here."

"But we can't just run in and start ordering Mr. Bin-Jazzi around. It's his place. He has to be polite, first."

"And where did *you* learn how to be polite?"

Dov looked around at the spice-souvenir-little-bit-of-everything shop.

Right here.

"How long did you say you lived here?" asked Natan.

"About six months, but it seems even longer."

"I *knew* there was something odd about you. You've been around too many Arabs and Messianics, whatever they call themselves."

"I told you—" Dov raised his finger in warning.

"All right." Natan waved his hands. "Don't get all excited again. But listen, I'm only here drinking Arab coffee in an Arab shop because it's the only way in. You're sure he's going to keep quiet about us? I noticed a few people watching us come in. And what about that lady?"

"Mr. Bin-Jazzi is my *friend.*"

"No, he's not. He's an *Arab.* And Jews don't have Arab friends these days."

"Spoken like a true warrior." Mr. Bin-Jazzi came up behind Natan and set down a tray with three steaming cups. Dov had almost forgotten how quietly the man could walk, like a cat. Natan nearly jumped through the ceiling. "But someday soon we will be neighbors again, yes?"

Natan narrowed his eyes and looked from Dov to the friendly shopkeeper, as if he had been betrayed already. They talked about the weather, the price of kerosene, and why the water seller no longer made his regular rounds. Natan said nothing. He sat with his arms folded, taking an occasional sip from his dark, thick Arab coffee, his eyes constantly on the door.

Dov tried to drink his coffee, too, even though there was no sugar to soften the bitter taste. He started to gag, but of course he could not be rude. So he closed his eyes and downed the cup.

"But I assume you didn't come here this afternoon to chat about the price of kerosene." After ten minutes Mr. Bin-Jazzi set down his cup, too. "Tell me why you came, then."

So Dov told him—leaving out some of the details about who his brother really was.

"You understand that if someone were to find out I allowed Jews through my tunnel . . ." Mr. Bin-Jazzi made a slicing motion across his throat.

"I'm sorry, *Abuna*." Dov used the Arab word for *father*. "I'm truly sorry. I won't ever ask again. And you know I've never told anyone about the tunnel."

"This I know." The man nodded. "After all, you see I am still alive."

Dov had to smile at Mr. Bin-Jazzi's gentle humor.

Natan was raking the walls with his eyes, searching for a tunnel opening.

You think you'll be able to find it, brother? Dov almost smiled. He was convinced Natan would have made his own way if he could have found the tunnel himself.

"However, one thing I must tell you, my friend." Mr. Bin-Jazzi's dark eyes looked serious as he took another sip of his coffee.

Dov nodded, as if he knew the warning to come. "People watch. You know I will not be able to help you like this again."

INTO THE OLD CITY

17

"Incredible!" Natan held his smoking candle up higher to get a better look at the ancient cistern tunnel that led them under the Old City between the Muslim and Jewish Quarters.

"This way." Dov paused for just a moment before picking his way through the tunnel. He knew the way too well through the old cisterns, room-sized vats where drinking water had been stored long ago. Over the rubble of Roman columns and cobblestones. And finally up the ladder and through the heavy door that led to the *yeshiva*.

"Is this the only way out?" whispered Natan. He needn't have bothered keeping his voice down.

Dov ducked his head to keep from being covered with dust. "It's the only way I know." He paused when the ladder trembled from an explosion up above. "But something's going on up there."

"Oh?" Another earsplitting boom shook their world. "Why do you say that?"

Dov didn't bother arguing with his sarcastic brother; he just pushed open the trapdoor that led into the closet of the Jewish boys' school. He'd been this way before, of course. But last time, he hadn't stepped into a war zone.

"Duck!" A shrieking whistle and a sickening explosion told Dov they were in the middle of trouble.

This is worse than at the windmill!

A ceiling beam collapsed, sending a shower of plaster and dust over their heads. Dov clutched his precious package and crouched in the darkness, trying to decide which way to go.

Natan grabbed him by the arm. "We've got to get out of here!" he shouted over the explosions.

Yes, but how? And to where? The attack on the yeshiva seemed to come from every direction, and to return to the tunnel might mean getting trapped there—perhaps forever.

"This way!" Natan darted first to the window, then to the door. All the chairs in the room were piled up against one wall, and most of the big oak tables had tumbled onto their sides. The ceiling now gaped open to the night air and the attackers all around them.

Behind them, another whistle and explosion turned the closet into kindling. Dov tried to move, but the crate slowed him down.

"Watch ou—" Natan didn't have time to finish his words; he just smothered Dov with his body as they both tumbled to the floor. The building trembled as if the outside walls would come crashing in, and shards of wood flew around them with tornado force.

A direct hit.

"Natan?" After a moment Dov dared whisper his brother's name, but Natan didn't move. "Natan, are you all right?"

Still, Natan didn't answer. By that time Dov could hear shouting outside on the streets. Jewish voices.

"Help!" Dov cried out, but he was afraid no one would be

able to hear his pitiful voice. The weight of his brother made it hard to get air. "Someone help me!"

With a surge of effort, Dov was able to squeeze out from underneath Natan's limp, clammy body. He felt the back of his brother's head, and his hand came back damp. That's when he knew that whatever had been meant to hit him, had hit Natan instead. A jagged piece of metal, perhaps, or a chunk of wood. Maybe it didn't matter.

"Don't die, Natan." Dov knelt by his brother and sobbed. What could he do now? "Please, God, don't let him die."

Natan's gun lay in the dust on the floor beside him. It didn't seem fair. This horrid metal thing had survived, when Dov's only family lay dying on the floor. Natan might be a dangerous terrorist, but Dov had searched for him too long to have him die so soon.

"No!" He picked up the gun with two fingers and flung it into the jumble of plaster and wood they had come from. It was the only protest he could think of—he no longer wanted anything to do with guns and bombs. The gun clattered and bounced to the bottom of its own grave in the ruined building, but it didn't make Dov feel any better. He knelt next to Natan's still body, shaking with anger.

Natan, the terrorist.

Natan, his brother.

Natan, the only family Dov had left.

"So I found him, God," he cried out. "Now what?"

As if God spoke from behind doors, the street entry burst open, screaming on one rusty hinge and partly collapsing from its own weight. Dov squinted and held up his free hand when a bright shaft of light hit him in the eyes.

"Who are *you*?" demanded a hoarse voice behind the flash-light—in Hebrew, at least. "And what are you doing in here?"

"I need help." Dov ignored the question. He could explain later. "*We* need help."

That is, if there still *was* a we. Dov was afraid to know whether his prayer for help was too late.

"I thought I told everyone to get out of this building." The dark, bearded man sounded as if he was in command as he knelt at Dov's side. And in the shadowy light of the flashlight, Dov could make out only the man's beard and that he was perhaps somewhere in his forties.

"We, ah . . ." Dov wasn't sure how much he could explain. "We came from the outside. But my brother. Is he—"

The man shined the flashlight on a wicked gash and a rising goose egg on Natan's head. He slipped a finger under Natan's chin and pressed against his neck.

"He's picked up a nasty blow, but he still has a pulse."

Dov sighed in relief, just as Natan moaned softly and tried to roll around.

"Dov?" Natan tried to sit up and hold his hand to his head at the same time. "Oh, my head feels as if it's been split open."

"Not so fast," said the man, and the harshness in his voice melted away a bit. "Sit up slowly. Now, are you two going to tell me what you're doing here?"

"You risked your life for me." Dov could hardly believe it as he helped his wounded brother sit up. "You risked your life."

"Don't get emotional about it." Natan tried to wave his helpers off, but the effort must have hurt too much, since he gave up. "You wouldn't have needed my help if you hadn't been dragging around that stupid radio."

"A radio?" Their rescuer snapped to attention and looked around. "We could use another radio."

"It's mine," explained Dov. "Shortwave. For broadcasting."

"So you're Haganah?" the man asked. "You look a little young."

"He's a *lot* young," Natan corrected him. "And I'm Irgun, not Haganah. My commander assigned me to come into the Old City and help out in the defense."

Their rescuer paused until Natan held out his trembling hand.

"I'm a weapons instructor. Natan Israeli. My little brother, Dov."

"Weapons instructor, eh? Where's your weapon?"

Natan's faced turned even more pale as he searched his pockets.

"I *had* it with me." He looked around at the floor. "It must have fallen out somewhere."

Dov's heart stopped, but he could not make himself say what he knew, or what he had done to the weapon.

"I see," said the man. "Well, Natan and Dov Israeli, welcome to the Jewish Quarter. My name is Shimon."

"We came in through the tunnel," Dov finally admitted. He decided not to correct the man about his last name—Dov Israeli didn't sound so bad, after all. "The tunnel, right over—"

Dov pointed to where the closet had been, and Shimon followed with his flashlight. All they could see was a ceiling-high pile of cement, rubble, and splintered beams.

"Well, it *used* to be over there," mumbled Dov. Now the entrance—and his only way out of the Jewish Quarter—was sealed like a tomb.

"Arab grenades opened up this entire building." Shimon scanned his light around the ruins. "It's not safe in here. We'd best get out, before—"

Almost as if someone had heard him, the horrible shrieking of mortar fire once more filled the air above their heads. Shimon snapped off his light, and they ducked away from the open hole in the roof.

"Can you walk?" Shimon asked Natan.

Natan nodded, but even in the shadowy light his face looked pasty and his forehead was caked in white dust. "I think so. But my gun . . ."

"You could stay here to look for it, but I wouldn't trade my life for a piece of hardware." Shimon almost grinned. "It's a good thing the real war hasn't started yet."

Dov hated to think of what the *real* war would be like, if this wasn't it. Never before in his life had he been so close to the line of fire.

"I'll take you to my uncle Herschel's house." Shimon held the broken door open, though it hardly needed the help. "He's always taking in strays."

Dov thought that was a good way to describe himself and Natan. *Strays.*

By the next evening, Dov had set up his transmitter in the back room of a crooked house on the Street of the Steps, in the shadow of the tall outside wall and about halfway between Zion Gate and Dung Gate. As Shimon had expected, the family there had welcomed the two strays. And they thought the radio was great entertainment, a break from the weariness of survival and the nightly Arab shellings. Three wide-eyed children sat in a circle on the floor, watching every move Dov made, not flinching when the shooting started up again.

"Don't get so close to the radio, Haviva," said middle-aged Uncle Herschel, the owner of the house. He looked up over thick glasses and an old, dog-eared copy of the *Midrash*, the

Jewish book of wise sayings from the rabbis.

"We won't, Uncle Herschel," replied the oldest of the trio, a bright-eyed girl named Golda. But still she scooted as close as she could.

"That's good enough. Thanks." Dov signaled to his older brother, who wore his bandage on the back of his head with pride, and whom Dov had persuaded to string a length of antenna wire across the room to the top edge of a windowsill—*Haganah* antenna wire, even!

Natan nodded and grumbled something about how many radio broadcasts it would take to win the war, but he carefully tied off the end of the wire before letting it go. After that he took up a position behind the girls and pretended not to care what happened next. Of course, if he didn't help with the radio, he would have to read the Midrash over Uncle Herschel's shoulder. Uncle Herschel had already tried to teach them both a few sayings.

"All right, I'm ready." Dov looked up at the small clock on the wall. Ten minutes to nine. Ten minutes before Anthony would usually take to the air. The children hushed at his words.

But he'd forgotten one thing. Dov turned quickly to his brother, microphone in hand.

"Natan, you know how to whistle, don't you?"

Nathan wrinkled his nose in confusion. "Whistle?"

"And you know the 'Hatikvah,' of course."

"Of course, but—"

"I can't whistle. You do it." Dov flipped a switch on his portable transmitter, held the microphone up to Natan's face, and nodded.

BROTHERS

18

At first Natan just stared at the microphone, his jaw hanging slack.

"You're on the air," whispered Dov.

Natan shook his head.

But when Dov nodded once more and pointed at the microphone, Natan frowned, took a deep breath, and delivered the opening musical notes, the signature of the Haganah broadcast.

Dov grinned and took his turn when his brother was finished. "This is a special broadcast of the Kol Hamegen Haivri, the broadcasting service of the Haganah." He kept his eyes on his brother as he spoke. "Coming to you from inside the walls of the Jewish Quarter of the Old City..."

Were Anthony and Rachel listening? Dov could only guess. And he imagined leaning out the small window and shouting loudly enough for them to hear him, over the Old City wall and across the Valley of Hinnom, up the hill to Number 3 Malki Street, on the edge of the Yemin Moshe.

Who had said that people in Yemin Moshe could hear the

155

pain of the Old City? Natan, of course. But not even Natan could yell as loudly as Dov.

Maybe they had just turned on their radio. Dov had to keep from smiling at the thought of Avi, probably falling over in his chair at their special broadcast.

And it was a good one, Dov thought to himself. Uncle Herschel rambled a bit when he told about the nightly shellings, about the orphans and food shortages and fear. But his voice was strong and clear, even when his eyes filled with tears. And even Natan listened, along with the three children on the floor. Dov held the microphone steady.

"B'yerushalayim ircha," whispered Uncle Herschel, closing his eyes and rocking quietly. He ended each of his stories with the same prayer. "And to Jerusalem, your city, may you return in compassion."

It already feels like we're a long way from Jerusalem. Emily leaned on the *Helgefjord*'s railing that evening and watched the distant moon rising over a dark smudge of mountains.

The island of Cyprus.

Nothing on this trip had turned out the way she'd expected so far. Nothing at all, from Miss Pettibone to Russian refugees. And now, with the ship's engine problems, it had taken them a day and a half just to cover the last one hundred miles to Cyprus. But oh well. As she watched tree-spotted Cyprus grow taller with each sea mile, somehow it didn't seem as bad as her governess had made it sound, back in the passenger lounge a few minutes earlier:

"I'm very sorry, Miss Emily, but tonight I don't care to hear radio programs with old men reciting Hebrew prayers. I don't suppose your father would approve now, would he?"

This time Emily had missed the beginning of the broadcast, so she had reluctantly allowed Miss Pettibone to snap off the radio.

"I promise you that if we ever get home alive," Bambi sighed, "I shall never set foot off British soil again, as long as I live! I certainly don't know why Mum and Dad ever advised me to go to Palestine."

Emily smiled when she remembered Bambi's words. It was just like her. But oddly enough, they also reminded Emily of another promise—one she herself had made to Dov.

"If there's ever any way to find your family . . . perhaps even your mother . . ."

She hadn't forgotten her words to Dov when he had shown up to claim Julian near her Jerusalem home. She had promised, after all, without any way of knowing how to keep such a vow. And now . . .

"If there's ever any way to find your mother . . ."

The words echoed in her mind as she listened to the sea sounds of waves below. She did know Dov's father had died on Cyprus in a British detention camp.

What about his mother?

"I'll do what I can."

Her promise had sounded good at the time. Noble, even.

But now she asked herself what she could really do on her own. And her prayer was answered in the silence of the sea rushing by.

I can't do it by myself. All right, then, Lord—what do you have waiting for me?

She took a deep breath, and the salty breeze carried with it the faint but clear scent of this distant island, of cedar-dotted hillsides and sweet green fields. In this night she could almost smell the promise that was not her own, but God's.

And Emily Parkinson smiled. She couldn't help feeling God was bringing her to this place for a reason.

When Dov switched off the microphone a few minutes later, Natan just stood still. Uncle Herschel's Hebrew prayer seemed to have taken on a life of its own. The words echoed in the small front room of the crooked house on the Street of the Steps.

"To Jerusalem, your city, may you return in compassion . . ."

Even the three children didn't move.

"Do you think anyone out there heard us?" Dov asked.

"They heard you." Natan nodded. "They heard you."

Dov said nothing else until a few minutes later, when they were coiling up the antenna wire and putting away Dov's equipment. Uncle Herschel had retired to his chair in the corner, and the three kids were playing with a top on the floor by the front door. Dov stared out the tiny window into the evening gloom—the window that faced the wall, the valley, and Yemin Moshe.

"Do you believe in prayer, Natan?"

"You mean, after listening to your radio broadcast?" Natan paused and scratched a half-week's stubble on his chin before answering. "You had me for a minute, there, I have to admit. But I don't know. I believe in me."

"That doesn't seem like enough. Not anymore."

"Maybe not." He lowered his voice. "But maybe hanging around those Messianics has toyed with your mind."

"They haven't toyed with anything. It's just they're the only people who make sense to me."

"What, including me?"

"Especially including you."

"Thanks a lot." But the bite was gone from Natan's words.

"Don't you see, Natan?" Dov pointed out at the darkness with his thumb as the sound of a lone shot echoed against the Old City walls. "Everything else out there is crazy. Too many Arabs wave their fists in the streets. And you Irgun are just as bad, maybe worse. Why do you hate each other so?"

"They started it." Natan answered in the flat, dull tone Dov had come to despise.

"Sure, but who cares who started it? Even if you *are* right, it doesn't matter. It doesn't make any sense. You hit them, they hit you back harder. And on and on. Where does it stop? Rachel and Anthony said . . ."

Dov's voice dropped off when he realized what he was about to say. Rachel and Anthony were always talking about the Messiah, and only now was it starting to make sense. Only now, behind these walls, in the middle of this crazy war in the making.

"Go ahead." Natan crossed his arms. "What did your Messianic friends have to say? And how about that crazy Arab shopkeeper?"

"I told you, he's not crazy. And I don't like it when you—"

Natan held up his hands. "Not another fight, okay? I'm not in the mood."

Neither was Dov.

But Natan wasn't quite finished. "Okay, listen, I don't care what you believe, Dov. Peace, the Messiah, or Father Christmas—whatever makes you feel better. But you can just leave me out of it.

"And I'll tell you something else, because you're my only kid brother and I wouldn't want to see you getting hurt." Natan looked around the room. "Don't bring up this peace stuff, this Messiah stuff . . . at least not with people around here, okay? They're likely to feed you to the lions—or the Arabs—if they hear you talking the way you do. It doesn't sound very Jewish."

Maybe true. Dov still wasn't sure how the pieces fit together, but he thought it might be as Jewish as anything he'd ever heard—maybe more. "Just one more question, Natan."

Natan sighed and adjusted his bandage. "All right, one more, and then do you promise to quit bothering me?"

"I'll try not to bother you," Dov told him. "I'm going back out, you know."

"Through your tunnel?" Natan laughed. "I don't think so."

"I'll find a way. But I just want to know: What do you think of the Wailing Wall?"

Natan looked at him as if perhaps his brother was the one who had been hit in the head. "Seriously?"

Dov nodded.

"It's a shrine. A . . . a special place. What do you mean, what do I think?"

"Just what I said. If it's so special, what makes it special?"

"That's more than one question."

"No, it's not. It's part of the first question. I want to know what you think: What makes the Wailing Wall special?"

"I don't know." Natan finally shrugged, but his voice was soft, as if he remembered something. "Abba always talked about coming here . . . to the wall. You probably don't remember. You were too little."

"I remember."

"It was part of Herod's old temple. Jews like to pray—"

"There." Dov stabbed at the air with his finger. "That's what I mean. You think that wall, this city, is worth defending, maybe with your life, don't you? The Wailing Wall is part of this place. You must think it's more than just a few blocks of stone. Otherwise, we Jews could just move to Tel Aviv, right?"

"Well, sure, this whole place is more than stones. But—"

"We have enemies on two sides, lobbing in bombs and shooting at us every night. We're surrounded. And still you wanted to come to the Old City."

"If you want to put it like that. But I don't see—"

"Do you want to know what was on the note I put in the wall not even two weeks ago?"

Dov's course change stopped Natan for a moment, but he recovered quickly. "Now, wait a minute. That wall is in Arab territory. There is no way you could have been there. You put a *note* in the wall?"

"I was there eleven days ago."

"Liar."

"You and I got through the Arab neighborhood, didn't we?"

"Barely."

Dov didn't say anything for a long moment, waiting for his brother to take the bait.

"All right." Natan sighed. "Tell me. What was in your note . . . your note to God?"

Satisfied, Dov rose to his feet. He'd made his point—the note and the Wailing Wall mattered to his brother. Natan believed more than he claimed to believe. And maybe so did Dov.

He was pretty sure of something else, too: Part of Mr. Bin-Jazzi's faith had rubbed off on him. Maybe part of Rachel and Anthony's faith, as well. At least, that's what it felt like. And strangely enough, Dov didn't mind. It felt as if he was starting to see things clearly, maybe for the first time.

"I can't tell you what was on the note," Dov replied at last. "All I can say is God answered the prayer."

Natan groaned.

Dov went on. "At first I didn't think He would. I was like you. But now I know. God answered my prayer."

With that, Dov headed for the door. He had plenty to do. He would check the radio transmitter's battery, make sure there was enough power left for another broadcast or two. He would try to think of something else to say for the next one. There were plenty of people here in the Jewish Quarter, people with stories, people he could interview.

"Hey, Dov, now I'm curious. You have to tell me what the prayer was. Listen, I'm your big brother! I order you to tell me. In fact . . ."

Dov smiled as he turned from the brother who was his answer to prayer. And he remembered what Rachel and Anthony had told him at their Sabbath table about saying things to make people thirsty so they would want to know more.

Try some salt, big brother. But that wasn't what Dov said.

"I'm glad I found you, Natan."

"You mean you're glad *I* found *you.*"

"Sure."

Natan paused for a moment, then added, "Me too, kid."

OF BOMBS AND PEACE

Because the PROMISE OF ZION books are historical fiction, combining real facts and events with made-up people and situations, the question always comes up: Where do the ideas for these books come from?

Some of the best sources for ideas for a book like this are the diaries of people who were really there. For example, the account of the attack on Kolonia in chapter eleven is based on an eyewitness account by a journalist named Harry Levin, from his book *Jerusalem Embattled: A Diary of the City Under Siege* (London, Victor Gollancz Ltd., 1950). The April 12 attack happened very much as described in *Brother Enemy*—from the course of the Jewish attackers, to the thirty-minute battle, to the account of the chicken!

Parts of the description of the Western Wall, or Wailing Wall, were taken from another first-person account, this one called *Forever My Jerusalem* by Puah Shteiner (Jerusalem, Feldheim Publishers, 1988). I found this special little book in a bookshop not far from the wall itself, in the Jewish Quarter. The neighborhood had once been a battleground in the fight for the Old City back in 1948. Mrs. Shteiner's account of her childhood years in the Jewish Quarter helped me add authentic details to my own observations of the Old City. After all, the area around the Western Wall looked quite different back in the 1940s, before the main plaza was cleared out following 1968's Six-Day War.

Two events inspired the account of the street bombing in this book in chapters five and six, and the account in our story borrows facts from both. The first was an explosion in which the offices of the *Palestine Post* newspaper were destroyed by a bomb-carrying army truck parked in front of the office on Sunday evening, February 1, 1948. According to a *Post* account the next day, the explosion rocked a large portion of the city and smashed windows and doors within a one-mile radius. The stubborn *Post* journalists were not put off by the explosion, however; they borrowed another press and worked all night to prepare the next day's edition.

A second blast destroyed much of Ben Yehuda Avenue, a popular shopping street, exactly three weeks later. Even bigger than the previous explosion, the Ben Yehuda blast brought down three- and four-story buildings and shattered shops for hundreds of meters. It also killed many people.

Through all the trouble, many of the British tried their best to keep order in a tough situation. But looking back today, it was not a bright moment for Britain. As the outgoing British High Commissioner Sir Alan Cunningham put it, "So much effort expended, so many lives lost to such little purpose finally. Thirty years and we achieved nearly nothing."

English, Irish, Palestinian, Jew . . . history seems to repeat itself. Despite cease-fires and peace negotiations, the fighting between Jews and Arabs goes on and on. And those problems that were left unsolved in 1948 keep bubbling to the surface today, like an infected sliver left under the skin. It is left for us, and the children of the survivors, to make peace and to pray for peace. As King David once wrote, we should "pray for the peace of Jerusalem: 'May those who love you be secure. May there be peace within your walls and security within your citadels.' For the sake of my brothers and friends, I will say, 'Peace be within you'" (Psalm 122:6–8, NIV).

FROM THE AUTHOR

The adventures don't stop with the last page of this book! Here are several ideas for you to try:

1. *Jump into the next adventure*, called *Freedom Trap*. Check out the preview at the end of this book. And I'm working on the sixth book in the series, too.

2. *Discover other books.* I've put together a list of some of my favorite books, magazines, Web sites, music, and more on Israel. They'll help you get a better feel for the strange and wonderful land Dov and Emily came to. Be sure to show this section to your parents or teacher.

3. *Write to me.* I always enjoy hearing from readers, and I answer all my mail. How did you like the book? Did you have a question about anything that happened, or about what the characters were thinking? What's next? My address is: Bethany House Publishers, 11400 Hampshire Avenue South, Bloomington, MN, 55438 USA.

4. *Go online.* Visit my Web site at *www.coolreading.com*. That's where you can pick up writing tips from your favorite authors, share your ideas online, or even review a book. There's plenty of cool stuff to do at coolreading! Check out *www.bethanyhouse.com*, too, for more of the latest news about PROMISE OF ZION and my other series.

That should keep you busy . . . until the next adventure.

Shalom!

Robert Elmer

WANT TO KNOW MORE?

You're in luck! The library, bookstands, and even the Internet are full of great resources for learning more about Israel and about the incredible events that happened there between 1946 and 1949. Here are a few ideas to get you started.

Picture Books on Israel

- *The Bible Lands Holyland Journey* by Dr. Randall D. Smith. Published by Doko in Israel, this is one of the better picture books of Israel and the Holy Land I've found. You'll see pictures of many of the places Dov and Emily visit.

History

- *Front Page Israel* by the *Jerusalem Post* (Jerusalem Post, 1986). This book contains copies of actual newspapers as they appeared between 1932 and 1986. It may be a little hard to locate, but this book is a treasure trove of real-life history.
- *Dawn of the Promised Land* by Ben Wicks (Hyperion, 1997). This book was written for Israel's fiftieth anniversary, and it's very good. It's not exactly a children's book, but there are lots of interesting interviews with people remembering what it was like to be a kid in the Promised Land in 1948, doing the kinds of things Dov and Emily did.
- *The Best of Zvi* by Zvi Kalisher. This man's story inspired many of the events in Dov Zalinski's life. In fact, I had a chance to interview him personally in his Jerusalem home.

What a story—truth is even more exciting than fiction! The book is available through the Friends of Israel Gospel Ministry in New Jersey, P.O. Box 908, Bellmawr, NJ 08099. They also have an interesting magazine called *Israel, My Glory.*

- *The Creation of Israel* by Linda Jacobs Altman (Lucent Books World History Series, 1998). A good all-in-one history of how Israel was founded; this book has a useful timeline, index, and pictures, too. A perfect resource for a student's research paper.

- *Child of the Warsaw Ghetto* by David Adler, illustrated by Karen Ritz. Some of the scenes in this picture book are sad and hard to take, but it gives an accurate idea of what people like Dov went through during the worst days of World War II.

Hebrew

Hebrew for Everyone, published and distributed by Epistle. Here's a fun, kid-friendly approach to learning the language of the Old Testament—and today's Israel! The study guide is written by Hebrew believers in Jesus and is designed for kids and beginners. You can learn the Lord's Prayer in Hebrew! I picked up my copy at the Garden Tomb in Jerusalem for twenty shekels. (A shekel is about twenty-five cents.) Contact Epistle at P.O. Box 2817, Petach Tikva, 49127, Israel.

Internet

- The International Christian Embassy of Jerusalem *(www.icej.org.il)* is a good place to connect to links for travel and historical information on Jerusalem and Israel.

- The U.S. Holocaust Memorial Museum *(www.ushmm.org)* is the leading museum in North America for information on what happened to the Jewish people before, during, and after World War II.

Music

- *Adonai—the Power of Worship From the Land of Israel* (Integrity Music). Good Messianic music that gives an excellent flavor of Hebrew-style worship songs. Includes the "Hatikvah," Israel's national anthem.

PREVIEW

Dov and Emily's adventures continue in book five of
PROMISE OF ZION, *Freedom Trap*.

Emily and Dov parted paths on the eve of Israel's independence, but Emily's journey is cut short when her ship home to England docks in Cyprus for emergency repairs. Could Dov's mother still be alive in one of the island's detention camps for illegal Jews?

Meanwhile, Dov—trapped in the siege of the Jewish Quarter—discovers purpose in his dangerous situation when Arab attacks leave a dozen orphans hungry and alone. Caught in circumstances beyond their control, can Dov and Emily trust God to help them find freedom?

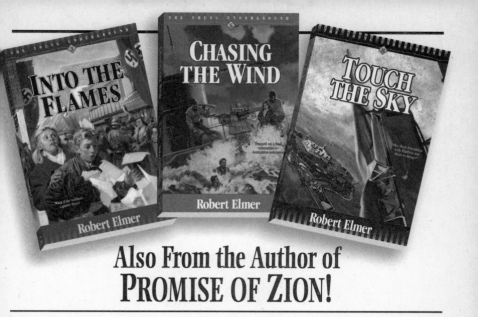

Also From the Author of
PROMISE OF ZION!

Boys and girls from all over the country write to Robert Elmer telling him how much they love THE YOUNG UNDERGROUND books—have you read them?

In THE YOUNG UNDERGROUND, eleven-year-old Peter Andersen and his twin sister, Elise, are living in the city of Helsingor, Denmark, during World War II. There are German soldiers everywhere—on the streets, in patrol boats in the harbor, and in fighter planes in the sky. Peter and Elise must help their Jewish friend Henrik and his parents escape to Sweden. But with Nazi boats patrolling the sea, they'll need a miracle to get their friends to safety!

Throughout the series Peter and Elise come face-to-face with guard dogs, arsonists, and spies. Together they rescue a downed British bomber pilot, search for treasure, become trapped on a Nazi submarine, and uncover a plot to assassinate the King of Denmark!

Read all eight exciting, danger-filled books in THE YOUNG UNDERGROUND!

A Way Through the Sea   *Chasing the Wind*
Beyond the River   *A Light in the Castle*
Into the Flames   *Follow the Star*
Far From the Storm   *Touch the Sky*

Available from your local Christian bookstores or from Bethany House Publishers.

The Leader in Christian Fiction!

BETHANY HOUSE PUBLISHERS

11400 Hampshire Ave. South
Minneapolis, MN 55438

www.bethanyhouse.com

Series for Middle Graders* From BHP

ADVENTURES DOWN UNDER · by Robert Elmer
When Patrick McWaid's father is unjustly sent to Australia as a prisoner in 1867, the rest of the family follows, uncovering action-packed mystery along the way.

ADVENTURES OF THE NORTHWOODS · by Lois Walfrid Johnson
Kate O'Connell and her stepbrother Anders encounter mystery and adventure in northwest Wisconsin near the turn of the century.

BLOODHOUNDS, INC. · by Bill Myers
Hilarious, hair-raising suspense follows brother-and-sister detectives Sean and Melissa Hunter in these madcap mysteries with a message.

GIRLS ONLY! · by Beverly Lewis
Four talented young athletes become fast friends as together they pursue their Olympic dreams.

MANDIE BOOKS · by Lois Gladys Leppard
With over five million sold, the turn-of-the-century adventures of Mandie and her many friends will keep readers eager for more.

PROMISE OF ZION · by Robert Elmer
Following WWII, thirteen-year-old Dov Zalinsky leaves for Palestine—the one place he may still find his parents—and meets the adventurous Emily Parkinson. Together they experience the dangers of life in the Holy Land.

THE RIVERBOAT ADVENTURES · by Lois Walfrid Johnson
Libby Norstad and her friend Caleb face the challenges and risks of working with the Underground Railroad during the mid–1800s.

TRAILBLAZER BOOKS · by Dave and Neta Jackson
Follow the exciting lives of real-life Christian heroes through the eyes of child characters as they share their faith with others around the world.

THE YOUNG UNDERGROUND · by Robert Elmer
Peter and Elise Andersen's plots to protect their friends and themselves from Nazi soldiers in World War II Denmark guarantee fast-paced action and suspenseful reads.

*(ages 8–13)